P9-CDC-498

Return to the Willows

Return to the Willows

JACQUELINE KELLY

Illustrations by **CLINT YOUNG**

HENRY HOLT AND COMPANY

New York

For Wayne Hollomon Price,
who encouraged me to write this book,
and who dreamt I conducted the 9th

—J. K.

For Dawn and Lily (my pencil and eraser),
who inspire my every line and erase away those that aren't perfect—
Thank you for believing in me.

—C. Y.

Henry Holt and Company, LLC
Publishers since 1866
175 Fifth Avenue
New York, New York 10010
mackids.com

Library of Congress Cataloging-in-Publication Data
Kelly, Jacqueline.
Return to the willows / by Jacqueline Kelly ;
illustrations by Clint Young.—1st ed.
p.   cm.
ISBN 978-0-8050-9413-8 (hc)
[1. Animals—Fiction.] I. Young, Clint, ill.
II. Grahame, Kenneth, 1859–1932. Wind in the willows. III. Title.
PZ7.K296184Re 2012   [Fic]—dc23   2011041298

First Edition—2012/Designed by April Ward
Printed in China by South China Printing Co. Ltd.,
Dongguan City, Guangdong Province
1 3 5 7 9 10 8 6 4 2

Return to the Willows

Being a respectful sequel to Mr. Kenneth Grahame's
The Wind in the Willows, containing helpful commentary,
explanatory footnotes, and translation from the
English language into American.

CHAPTER ONE

Our Story Begins

*In which those of us who are familiar with the Rat and Mole hail them as old friends.
And for those of you who aren't, well, you should put this book down right away and
ask your librarian for the first book so you won't be entirely clueless. (Oh, all right.
You can come along if you promise to keep up, but no moaning about being lost.)*

The Mole and Water Rat drifted along the River in a tiny blue-and-white rowboat. The current gurgled and chuckled, delighted with its comrades for the day. The sun smiled down upon our heroes and gladdened their hearts; the lightest of zephyrs ruffled their fur. There was not a hawk in the sky, and even the dark fringe of the Wild Wood glowering in the distance could not cast a pall upon the shining hour.

The Rat pulled on the oars every now and then but mostly let the River do the work, for he was busy composing poems in his head, rhyming "dream" with "stream," that sort of thing. The Mole had brought along a good book to read (for it is a firm and fast rule that one should never leave one's burrow without a good book in hand), and was deeply immersed in the adventures of a young girl who'd fallen down a rabbit hole. The hole was unlike any the Mole had ever visited—and he had visited any number of them in his time, for he counted a great many rabbits among his friends—but he was enjoying it immensely, as he was very fond of all stories that took place underground. He leaned back upon a plump cushion and wiggled his toes in sheer happiness.

From time to time, the Rat auditioned a new ditty by speaking it aloud, to see whether it lived and breathed in the open air, or withered and died as so many rhymes do when they are first introduced to the world. (It is a strange fact that many of those rhymes which ring true in the composer's head will, when spoken aloud, limp and wheeze in the most pathetic manner, and are best put out of their misery right away.[1])

Really, sighed the Mole to himself, the day was perfect. Or at least it would be, if only the Rat would stop interrupting his reading.

Honestly, thought the Rat, the day was ideal. Or at least it would

_____

1. Reader, while it's true that there's nothing better in the world than *good* poetry, there's also nothing worse than *bad* poetry.

be, if only the Mole would put down his book and pay proper attention.

"Moly, listen here. Can you think of a word that rhymes with balloon? The only thing I can come up with is mushroom, and that doesn't work at all. One should avoid fungus in poetry, as a rule."

With great reluctance, Mole tore himself away from an intriguing chapter about a frightfully odd tea party, in which two of the characters were trying to stuff a third into the teapot. The thought of a dormouse bobbing about in the tea struck the Mole as a shockingly shabby way to treat a guest, to say nothing of unhygienic.

He said, "Why do you need a rhyme for balloon?"

The Rat looked at him incredulously and said, "Haven't you heard? Why, it's the talk of the River. Toad's grown bored with boats, and his motor-car craze is fading, so now he's gone out and bought himself a—"

"Yoo-hoo!" came a gleeful familiar voice. It sounded very much like their friend Toad, but he was nowhere to be seen. Toad's voice was present, but Toad, in the flesh, was not.

"What nonsense is he up to now?" said the Rat, frowning. "He really is a most provoking creature."

"Hulloo, hulloo! Up here, you two!" sniggered the invisible Toad. "I'm up here!"

A passing cloud momentarily blotted out the sun. The two looked up to see that the cloud was not in fact a cloud, but rather a huge yellow balloon sailing overhead, a majestic airship, as shocking as another sun in the sky. The Mole gasped, and his heart skittered in his chest, for he'd never seen anything so splendid in all his life.

Suspended in the wicker basket below the balloon, waving and hullooing at them, was the familiar podgy form of Toad.

"As I was about to say," said the Rat drily, "he's bought himself a brand-new balloon, and I hear it cost the earth. Shall we place a bet on how long *this* phase lasts?"

The Mole ignored him, fixated as he was on the enormous globe. He clasped his paws together and breathed, "Oh, my."

"Hoy, you two, what d'you think?" yelled Toad, his voice growing fainter as a current of wind spirited him away. "Ain't she a beaut? I'll take you fellows for a ride one day, if you like."

The Mole could barely make out these last few words. But they stuck in his brain and lodged in his heart.

The Rat chattered on, making rude comments about Toad's passing manias and how they never lasted and how he was sure to come to grief this time, and that he—Rat—only hoped that he—Toad—didn't take some innocent victim with him when it happened, as it was bound to. For although Toad was in many respects a fine fellow, he possessed (let's face it) a light and volatile character, and trailed catastrophe in his wake at every turn, and was not to be trusted with conveyances of *any* kind, and so forth and so on.

The Mole, his book long forgotten in his lap, ignored him. Eyes agleam, mouth agape, he stared at the balloon until it shrank to a speck on the horizon.

"Mole?" Ratty examined him with astonishment and not a little alarm, for the Mole's expression was one the Rat had seen before, specifically on the visage of Toad when he'd first laid eyes on a motor-car, and been swept up in his craze for speed and the pull of the open road. "Moly?"

"Hmm?" said the Mole.

"Mole, old fellow, whatever's come over you?"

The Mole said, "Hmm? What was that?"

"Now, look here," said the Rat severely, "if you're thinking of bal-looning with Toad, you've got to put that idea right out of your head. He's not competent to operate a tricycle, let alone a flying machine. Good heavens, man, you'd be taking your life in your hands!"

The Mole's expression changed, and his eyes regained their focus. "I s'pose you're right, Ratty. You're always right about that sort of thing. Still, it must be nice . . ." His voice trailed off for a moment, but then he rallied and said, "Never mind. Messing about in boats is more than enough for me."

A swift flitted by overhead, carving the sky into invisible loops with its acrobatics. It glanced at the boat and then, disbelieving its own eyes, swooped and circled back, landing lightly on the bow. The bird cocked its head and surveyed the tiny vessel's passengers.

"My word," chirruped the Swift, "it *is* a mole after all. A Water Rat is to be expected, but a Water *Mole*? I thought my eyes were playing tricks on me."

"Good morning, Swift," said Mole. "Ratty has introduced me to the pleasures—nay, the joys! of the nautical life. He's taught me how to row and swim, and I'm here to tell you that there is nothing, simply nothing, so grand as messing about in boats."

"That may be true," retorted the Swift, "but it isn't a natural state for a ground dweller such as yourself."

"Natural or not," said Ratty stoutly, "my friend here is every bit at home on the River as I am. He's quite an expert on the life aquatic."

The Swift ignored this and continued, "You don't see fish burrowing in the ground, do you? Leastways, not any self-respecting fish with a lick of common sense. *Ergo,* moles should not swim, or float about in boats, for that matter.² Since you, sir, are plainly a mole, your job is to grub about in the earth. You were born and bred for it, and that's all there is to it. Why, next you'll want to fly, and all of Nature will be set on its head, topsy-turvy. It ain't natural, I tell you."

And with that, the Swift launched himself into the air and flew away before the Mole could think of a suitably crushing retort. (Mole, despite his many sterling qualities, was not always the most nimble-witted creature when it came to composing the withering riposte.)

"What colossal cheek!" Rat said. "Don't let that bird bother you, Moly. He's just jealous." Rat went on about it at length and even threw in some harrumphing noises until his friend felt better.

Toad's magic words, "I'll take you fellows for a ride . . . for a ride . . . ," grew louder in the Mole's head; his imagination swirled

---

2. *Ergo*: Latin for "therefore." The Swift is being a show-off, and nobody likes a show-off.

with visions of the dazzling yellow aircraft. Who could've imagined that such a machine existed? Even better, that the whole point of its existence was to make flight possible for earthbound beings, including modest tillers of the humble soil? As in, let us say, moles? As in, for example, one mole in particular? Why should those lucky creatures who'd been blessed with wings be the only ones to soar and swoop and glide and dip?

He picked up his book and soon appeared to be engrossed in his reading, but if the Rat had been paying more attention, he would have noticed that his friend did not turn a single page throughout the rest of their excursion.

CHAPTER TWO

The Wild Blue Yonder

In which one of our heroes achieves his heart's desire.
And then wishes he hadn't.

Perhaps it was the stimulating effect of the flourishing season, or possibly the rankling remark made by the Swift about ground grubbers, but whatever the cause, the Mole was a changed animal. He found himself unable to concentrate on much of anything other than the brilliant balloon. What must it be like to glide on high with the birds and the clouds? In short, why should swifts (and toads) have all the fun?

With this in mind, the Mole trotted to Toad Hall one bright afternoon and found the owner on the great velvety expanse of lawn with his balloon almost fully inflated. The Mole caught his breath at the magnificence of it.

"Hullo, Moly," Toad called out. "I'm just about to take off. Come along with me. There's absolutely nothing like it! The fresh air! The grand views! When I think of all the time I squandered on trivial pursuits such as boating, I'm almost reduced to tears. Why would anyone choose to spend his time floating on the River when he could spend it sailing in the Air? And as for motoring? Pah!"

"Well, I . . ." Mole found himself suddenly tongue-tied, now that his dearest wish was about to be realized.

"Oh, do come along, Mole, it's perfectly safe with an experienced balloonist like myself at the helm. Why, I've been doing it for days now. Absolutely nothing to it. Jump aboard, Mole, there's a good chap." He added, "Cook packed me a first-rate lunch. There's plenty."

"All right," said Mole shyly.

"Good man! That's the spirit! Just let me check the wind gauge, and we'll be on our way in a tick."

Mole clambered into the basket, which creaked alarmingly, even more so when Toad joined him.

Mole said nervously, "Are you sure it will hold us both?"

" 'Course it will. It's the best model on offer." Toad fiddled with the valves, and the coal gas flared up with a mighty *whoosh*.

"Toad!" cried Mole, recoiling in horror. "It's on fire!"

" 'Course it's on fire. It's supposed to be on fire. You burn the gas, and that makes the air hot, and that's what goes into the balloon, and that's what lifts it all up. At least, I *think* that's how it works. Silly me, I never can keep it straight."

With no further preamble, the balloon, the basket, and its inhabitants sprang from the earth. The Mole gasped in terror and clutched the rim of the basket as the ground receded beneath them at a horrifying clip. His instincts screamed that he'd made a dreadful mistake, that it was all so terribly wrong. That the proper situation for a mole—the *only* situation for a mole—was to remain firmly affixed to the earth or, better yet, *under* the earth in his own familiar burrow. What had he been thinking? He sank to the bottom of the basket and cowered there, his stomach heaving.

"Mole, old thing, whatever's the matter?" said Toad. "You're missing the view."

Mole moaned, his face hidden in his paws, "Take me home, Toad. Oh, please, take me home."

"Don't be ridiculous, we've only just started. We won't be home for hours yet. Here, stand up and look at the Hall. There's the orchard, and there's the croquet lawn, and there's the boathouse. Oh, and look, there's Cook in the kitchen garden, waving her tea towel at us.

Hullooo!" Toad waved vigorously, causing the basket to sway and the Mole to gulp. "Stand up and take a look, Mole. Hullooo!"

Mole pleaded, "Oh, Toad, you've got to steer it back."

"Steer it, did you say? Don't be absurd, there's no *steering* it, old thing. No, no, not at all. That's part of the charm, old fellow, part of the adventure. To sail wherever the currents take one. To surrender one's course to the vagaries of the wind. Why," Toad chuckled, "I s'pose that's where the phrase 'to throw caution to the wind' comes

from. I've never thought of that before. Have you ever considered that, Mole?"

There was no answer.

"Moly?"

There was still no answer.

"What are you doing down there," inquired Toad, "all curled up like a hedgehog?"

"I want to go home," murmured the pitiful Mole. "I want my own little burrow, even if it is just a hole in the ground. I want to dig and tunnel and rummage about in the earth. The Swift was right. It's what a mole *does*, Toad. It's simply not natural for moles to fly."

"Stuff and nonsense," Toad protested. "By your reasoning, it's not natural for toads to fly either, but look at me. Here I am. Free as the proverbial bird on the wing. I must say, you disappoint me, Mole. I never took you for such an old fuddy-duddy. Where's your sense of adventure? I, Toad, crave the Life Adventurous. Oh, look, there's the village and the church. And there's a flock of sheep grazing on the commons. They look like balls of cotton from here. And, look, there's the River." Toad prattled on and pretended not to notice Mole bundled in his misery.

"I say," exclaimed Toad. "I wonder if that's the meadow where your burrow is. It's rather hard to tell from here."

Mole uncurled himself at these tantalizing words.

Toad went on. "Shame that I can't tell for certain. Ah, well. It's too bad you're missing this once-in-a-lifetime opportunity, Moly."

The Mole cautiously raised his head.

Toad continued, "It's not every day that one gets to see one's home from such a lofty perspective. Ah, well."

Mole spoke in a small voice. "D'you really think it might be my meadow?"

"Difficult to say. I imagine that only someone familiar with the area could tell. I can take us down a bit lower, for although you can't, technically speaking, *steer* the aircraft, you can make it go up or down easily enough."

The Mole squeezed his eyes shut, gripped the side of the basket, and slowly pulled himself to a standing position, trying hard not to jiggle the aircraft. Right, Moly, he told himself sternly, you can do this. He willed himself to look.

Below him, as far as the eye could see, lay the overwhelming panorama of the wide world: meadows of barley neatly divided by the darker lines of hedges and roads, an undulating checkerboard of emerald green and lime green and pale gold. Dotted across the pastoral landscape were charming hamlets, including their own familiar village of Toadsworth, punctuated by the steeples of picturesque churches. The Mole was entranced. He exclaimed, "Oh, my!" and would have clapped his paws together in excitement, except that doing so would have meant releasing his hold on the basket.

He contemplated the countryside in awe. In the distance lay the Wild Wood, lowering and sullen, even in full daylight. And there flowed the River, snaking its way through the scenery, shining like a mirror at the turns where it caught the sun. Mole was agog, which gratified his host no end.

"Isn't it grand?" proclaimed Toad. "I'm not the sort to say I told you so, but I did tell you so.[3] There's absolutely nothing like it. Here, let's drop down and see if it's your meadow." He pulled on the release valve.

They sank slowly until Mole could see that the countryside was imprinted with a crazed web of dozens of narrow crisscrossing trails, along which many miniature gray shapes darted. Mole squinted, and the darting gray shapes turned into rabbits.

"I *think* it's my meadow," he said doubtfully. "It's all so different from up here. If only I could pick out a landmark."

A bird careered by and called out a greeting to Toad. Catching sight of the Mole, it uttered a squawk of disbelief. It was the very

---

3. Try and avoid telling people so. They don't like it, and it will win you no friends.

same Swift of earlier acquaintance. He landed on the rim of the basket and affixed the Mole with a beady gaze.

"I don't believe it!" he said. "You there, Mole, you are a creature out of place. It's most unnatural, this business. First the water, now the air. I shall have to report you to . . . to the authorities."

"Oh?" retorted Mole cheekily. "And who might that be?"

The Swift struggled with this and finally said, "Surely there's a . . . a bureau of something or other I can complain to. And you, Toad, I'm surprised at you for encouraging this sort of behavior in others. Bad enough that you're up here where you don't belong."

"Bilge," declared Toad. "And if you're going to ride with us, at least be polite about it. Otherwise, be off with you."

Once again Mole's brain hummed feverishly to produce a clever reply, but once again the Swift was gone before he could deliver up some sizzling repartee. (Just as well, for not all rudeness needs to be returned, measure for measure. Sometimes one just has to take the high road of good behavior, even if one is elbowed onto that path by the bad behavior of others.)

"Oh, look!" Mole cried, and pointed at a tiny boat on the River with an even tinier figure plying the oars. "Could that be Ratty? Hullooo, Ratty!" he called, but the figure took no notice. "Up here!" He momentarily forgot himself and waved vigorously, which sent the basket jig-jogging sideways. He grabbed the rim in a panic. And then, after taking a few deep steadying breaths, he let go again. He surveyed the world below him, and thought . . . *Yes.*

Yes, there was something to this ballooning business after all, with the fresh air in one's face, and the ripple of the bellying silk, and the faint creak of the basket. *Yes.* He raised his snout to taste the breeze and was shocked and enchanted to find alluring clues to a thousand and one tales unknown to him, whole volumes of information he'd never read before. There—yes, just *there*—came the faintest fragrance of strange wildflowers; from over there wafted the damp piney smell of unexplored forests; from there, the intriguing smell of murky marshes teeming with exotic life. And there was a hint of something else tickling his nose. Something briny that he'd never smelled before. Why should the air smell of salt? What could it be?

Mole sniffed deeply and pondered this thrilling question while Toad investigated the contents of the luncheon basket. Our aeronauts' attention was not focused on their course as closely as it should have been, so that neither one of them noticed they were drifting toward Toadsworth at a lower-than-recommended altitude.

The bewitched Mole said, "What is that smell, Toad, the one far off in the distance? That odd, particular smell that's . . . well . . . like salt?"

Toad paid him no attention. He was busy pawing through various wax-paper parcels and working himself into a snit. "Oh, drat," he grumbled peevishly. "Cook forgot to pack me a bottle of black currant cordial. What a bother. She knows it's my favorite. I'll have to speak to her about it."

"But that smell," Mole went on. "Why should the air smell like pickling brine?"

"Oh, here it is," said Toad, extracting a bottle swathed in straw. "Hmm? Oh, they tell me that's the Ocean, although I've never seen it."

"So that's the Ocean," said Mole in wonder. "I've read about it in books. They say it's a place where all the water in the world ends up, every stream and lake, every drop of rain. Do you think that includes our own River?"

"I s'pose," said Toad, unwrapping a packet of sandwiches. "Dig in, old thing."

Mole stared into the distance and said, "I wonder what it looks like, this Ocean?"

"They tell me it's huge. Water as far as the eye can see. And big waves, *enormous* waves. And terrible tides, and p'tickly nasty weather."

"Oh," said Mole diffidently, "but it does smell so very interesting. I think I'd like to see it one day, just for a little while. Could we get there by balloon, d'you think?" For Mole, having overcome his initial fear, had decided that ballooning was quite the way to go.

"Not really a place for Riverbankers," said Toad. "I say, do you want the cheese or the roast bee—"

His words were interrupted by a tremendous thump and a hair-raising screech, followed by the appalling sight of some kind of harpoon thrusting its way upward through the bottom of the basket.

"What's happening? What's happening?" yelled Toad.

The Mole danced out of the way of the sharp metal point as it rose between them until it loomed over their heads.

"What is it?" cried Toad.

The Mole took a tentative step closer and examined the strange object which had so ignominiously impaled their airship. "Oh, no," he moaned. "We've come down on the steeple."

CHAPTER THREE

Down to Earth

In which Mole learns an important lesson,
and Toad, being Toad, does not.

Toad exclaimed, "The steeple? That's ridiculous! We've got miles of room. . . ." He waved his paw and looked about him, and his voice trailed off, for indeed they were lodged—embarrassingly so—on top of the Toadsworth church. Below them, a gaggle of excited animals was already gathering on the cobblestones, for the sleepy village was generally short on such electrifying entertainment. The more sympathetic souls clasped their paws in consternation, while others of harder character nudged one another and snickered.

"Oh," groaned Toad, "my lovely balloon. What'll we do now, Moly?

Should I turn *up* the gas? Or should I turn *down* the gas? I just can't think."

"Don't touch the gas! Don't touch a thing!" shouted the Mole. "As far as I can tell, we're stuck. We have to climb down somehow and send for a wagon to collect the balloon." He was most cross with Toad, who was, after all, the pilot in charge.

Toad heard the ire in his friend's voice and deemed it unfair. "It was the wind, you know. Not my fault at all. I did warn you there's no steering these things."

"Oh, blast," fumed Mole. "You're absolutely right, Toad. It's actually all my fault for putting myself in your hands in the first place. Ratty tried to warn me, and he was absolutely right. Any creature with the slightest sense would have recognized it for a bad idea. Last year there were boat smashes, then there were car crashes, and now we have this. Oh, yes, the signs were there, all right, but did I heed them? No, I did not!" The Mole ranted away in severe tones about his own lack of judgment.

Toad listened in astonishment, for he had never seen the normally placid Mole so angry. On the other hand, he, Toad, had never been let off the hook so easily. But after listening to the Mole berate himself for a full minute, Toad began to feel decidedly uncomfortable. After yet another minute, Toad couldn't stand it anymore and, being a decent sort at heart, burst out with, "Moly, old fellow, please don't be so cross with yourself. It's all my fault, really, every single bit of it, and I'm terribly sorry." Tears brimmed in his pleading eyes. "I'm a very silly Toad. Can you ever forgive me?"

The Mole swallowed a bitter retort and sighed heavily. "Toad, we both should have watched where we were going. There's no use standing around dividing up the blame. It doesn't help us in getting down from here. We've got to abandon ship."

"Er," said Toad nervously, "how do we do that?"

"You do have a length of rope somewhere, don't you?"

"Erm, yes . . . but why?"

"We've got to climb down, of course."

Toad turned pale. "Are you sure, Moly? It's just that I'm, well"—his voice dropped—"you might not guess this about me since I'm otherwise extraordinarily athletic . . . but mountaineering's not really my sport, you see. I'm not a terribly keen climber."

Mole fished about and found a coil of rope. "Well, you're going to become one now—or perhaps you'd rather live out the rest of your days up here. How long d'you think those sandwiches will last you?"

Toad turned paler. Mole made several knots in the rope and secured it to the basket. He threw the length over the side. Looking down, he could see that it stopped far short of the ground. Dismay wrinkled his brow as he considered their plight. The rope was only long enough to get them to the roof. But it would have to do.

On the street below, a family of hedgehogs (who had considerably more sense than the rabbits and squirrels) had run home and fetched a bedspread and were now holding it stretched wide in case of catastrophe. Mole suppressed a shudder and said, "Come on, Toady, I'll go first. Just follow me and do what I do. And remember: Don't. Look. Down."

Toad moaned, "Moly, I don't think I can do it."

" 'Course you can," said Mole, "for the simple reason that you *have* to. Now, come along." The Mole eased himself over the rim and began to lower himself down the knotted rope, assiduously avoiding looking at the ground. He said, "Are you coming, Toad?"

A faint whimper issued from the basket.

"Toad!" snapped Mole, whose nerves were stretched to the breaking point. "Come along this instant!" Toad, his eyes bulging in fear, peered over the rim. Mole glared at him and said, "Don't make me come back up there."

Toad mutely shook his head and remained stuck fast.

Mole, who was now halfway down the rope, realized that threats were inadequate to the job. He made the decision to alter his tactics (not easily done when one is concentrating on climbing down a steeple) and employ the use of embarrassment as a corrective tool. "I know I warned you not to look down, Toad, but I've changed my mind. Look down and tell me what you see."

Toad stared at the gawking throng. A couple of the younger rabbits, under the impression that this was all some delightful amusement staged just for them, waved at him cheerfully.

"The whole village must be down there by now," said Mole. "And what do you think they're doing?"

Toad shook his head.

"Why, they're all staring at you. They're talking about you, every single one of them. And what do you think they're going to say tomorrow when they come back after breakfast and find you're still in the basket?"

Toad looked at Mole uncertainly.

"Oh, I can just hear them now," said Mole.

Toad frowned.

"Can you?" said Mole.

Toad frowned harder.

"They'll be laughing about it for years."

Thunder settled on Toad's brow; grim was his expression.

"They're probably making book about how long you'll be stuck up here."[4] Mole lowered himself the last few feet onto the slate roof, and before he could dust himself off, he was joined in a flash by Toad. A distant cheer rose from the crowd.

"So," said Mole, "I'm glad you decided to come along after all."

Toad, gasping for breath, said, "Thought you might need my help." He looked with dismay at the ground, still some distance below. "What do we do now, Moly?"

The Mole cast about and spied a series of gutters, which drained into a downpipe. "We'll just have to go down that drain. I can't see any other way."

Toad gnawed his lip. "Are you sure?"

"I'll go first. Follow me and do what I do."

The Mole crouched down and began to crawl along the lead gutter where it met the roof, the terrified Toad crowding him from behind. The soft lead gutters sagged alarmingly beneath their combined weight. Mole broke into a sweat.

"Toad," he rasped, "I know I told you to follow me, but we're too heavy together. Stay well back."

"Shan't," wheezed Toad.

---

4. Making book: taking bets. Now aren't you glad you've got helpful commentary? You probably thought you didn't need it, right?

Mole spoke through gritted teeth. "You are. A very. Provoking. Animal." The gutter protested under them. The noise so alarmed the Mole that he practically scampered the rest of the way to the down-pipe, Toad hard on his heels. They caught their breath, and Toad waved to the onlookers. He was rewarded with a faint huzzah.

"Stop playing to the crowd," chided Mole. "This is serious business."

But there was no worse encouragement to Toad's vanity than the attention of an adoring crowd. He bowed deeply. The next second, he lost his balance, uttered a strangled cry, and for one terrible moment teetered on the edge of the roof, frantically windmilling his arms.

The Mole made a sudden grab for his coattails and saved him from a certain plunge to the ground. The audience made an *ooohi*ng sound and gave the Mole a hearty round of applause.

"Do stop flailing about," said Mole. "We've got to concentrate on getting down from here in one piece."

"S-sorry," stammered the chastened Toad, and truly meant it. The Mole had just saved his life, and one should always be appreciative about such things.

"Right," said Mole. "We've got to negotiate this downpipe. Hold tight with all fours and lower yourself as if you're climbing down a tree. I'll go first. And for heaven's sake, don't push me this time."

Mole held on to the gutter and eased himself backward over the edge. The downpipe, having been in the sun all day, was uncomfortably hot to the touch. He lowered himself and was most of the way to the bottom when he looked up to see Toad sliding down the pipe toward him at an alarming rate.

"Grab hold, Toad. Slow down!"

"I can't! It's too hot."

Fortunately, they were only a foot or two from the ground when the Toad's feet collided with the Mole's head, causing our heroes to land in a tangle of limbs. Mole gingerly massaged his aching scalp while Toad bowed and saluted the cheering assembly.

Mole eventually managed to drag him away, and together they begged a ride to Toad Hall in the back of a coal wagon. Toad spent the ride bragging to the coal man about his own derring-do, and how he'd masterminded the hair-raising descent from the steeple. "And then I realized," he nattered on, "that the only way down was by rope. Fortunately, I, Toad, am a terribly keen climber. I, Toad, am a gifted athlete. One of those fortunate beings whom Nature has blessed with both strength and agility. To say nothing of supple grace. And quick wits. Even Mole here (who's not bad with a rope himself) learned a thing or two from me today. It's too bad he blundered into my path on the final descent and ruined what would have been a perfect landing.

I did warn him to get out of the way, but instead he sprained my foot with his head, and now I have this dreadful injury. But no matter, for I am cut from stalwart cloth. . . ."

Such was the Mole's reward for all his courageous service that day.

Our adventurers finally made it home, filthy, sunburned, exhausted. The first thing Toad did was to send a message for a crack team of salvage squirrels to retrieve the balloon. Mole, while outwardly commiserating about the damage to the airship, was inwardly content, for he had gone into the lists, done combat with his fears, and overcome them.[5] Valiant, doughty creature!

Now, if he could only think of what to tell Ratty.

---

5. This is a metaphor, a figure of speech, in which you say one thing but actually mean another in order to describe it in a new and colorful way. The lists are the fields where knights jousted, waving their lances and thundering at each other on great, heavy horses. Therefore, to say that one is going into the lists means that one is facing a difficult trial.

CHAPTER FOUR

The May Fair

In which our heroes celebrate the arrival of summer,
and two of them taste grief, although of different flavors.

The frisky Mole trotted along the path to the River, pausing now and then to admire a daisy here and snuffle at a lily of the valley there. He was in the finest mood, for not only was it the day of the May Fair, but the Rat had left his tiny boat at the landing for him so that he could float down to his friend's house in ease and comfort. (Toad had managed to resurrect his balloon, but Mole had sworn off flight forever, even if it meant never seeing the Ocean.)

"Good old Ratty," he said. "So considerate of others. Always thinks of his friends, Ratty does. Unlike some other creatures I could think of. Such as toads."

Now, while it was true that the pleasure of Toad's company was best appreciated in small doses, no sooner had Mole admitted this to himself than he felt a flush of shame, for he was a thoroughly decent sort and disliked speaking ill of neighbors (even those who might genuinely deserve it). He resolved to look for the best in Toad, who did have—in spite of his essential Toadness—a *few* endearing qualities.

Mole stepped lightly into the boat and loosed the painter the way Ratty had taught him.[6] A moment later, he was on his way.

The Mole looked forward to the day when he might have his own tiny boat cunningly fitted with comfy cushions and gleaming brass appointments. He would name it . . . he would name it . . . *Mole's Boat.* Oh, dear, how dreadfully unimaginative.[7] No, that wouldn't do at all. A delightful little boat called out for a delightful little name. He mulled this over but could not come up with something suitable. Never mind. The day was too fine to be taxing one's brain with such matters. The breeze, shuttling merrily back and forth along the banks, set the rushes to singing and the reeds to clacking in joyous

---

6. This is not what you think it is. In matters nautical, a painter is a rope attached to the bow of a boat.

7. Mole is absolutely correct about this.

counterpoint: *The first of May! The first of May! All creatures shall give thanks this day!* Before he knew it, he caught sight of the canted willow that marked the Rat's snug bijou residence under the bank.

"Hullo, Mole!" Rat hailed him from his doorway as Mole secured the boat.

"Hullo, Ratty. What a fine day for the Fair."

"The finest. Half a mo'— I'm almost ready." Ratty finished sleeking back his brilliantined fur with a pair of silver brushes. "Right," he said. "We're off."

The pair clambered up the shady bank and emerged into the marshy meadow. In the full sunlight, the Mole's new waistcoat glowed an alarming orange hue not often seen in Nature. The Water Rat looked startled and then studied his friend's new togs with a narrowed eye and furrowed brow.

"What is it, Ratty?" asked Mole.

After a moment, the Rat replied, "Oh, nothing. It's just . . ."

"Is your tummy paining you? You've got that look you get when you've been a greedy beggar and eaten too much."

"It's just . . . I say, old chap, are you actually going to wear that waistcoat?"

The Mole looked down at his new apparel. "What, this?" he said, an undertone of hurt creeping into his voice. "Is it too loud, do you think?"

The Rat, a kind and perspicacious animal, heard the dismay in his friend's voice and hurried to put things right. "No, no, old man, it's perfectly fine. It's new, isn't it? And such a bright, cheerful color. What d'you call it?"

"The tailor called it Canary Mélange," said Mole, doubtfully.[8]

"Well, well," said Rat. "Canary Mélange. So very . . . natty. So very . . . festive."

"The tailor *did* say it's the latest thing," said Mole, gathering his courage.

"Ah. Well. The very latest thing. Sets off your coloring so nicely. Now, come along, old thing. Quick march," ordered Ratty. "We don't want to miss out on any of the festivities."

They set off, the Mole silently berating himself. What a *blind* mole he was! *Why* had he allowed the tailor to talk him into Canary Mélange, when a part of him—the sensible part—had known better all along? Why hadn't he stuck to his usual choice, a sedate gray-and-white check? He fretted like this for a while, but the day was too deliriously fine for him to remain upset for long, and he soon got over himself.

They strolled through the lush water meadow swarming with

---

8. Reader, be not afraid. *Mélange* is a fancified French word that actually has a very simple meaning: the mixing of colors together. The French are always doing things like that, insisting on using a fancy word when a plain one will do nicely, thank you very much.

bejeweled dragonflies; they passed adjoining fields of thrusting green barley and soon came to a well-worn path that ran along the hedgerows. All the small society of the undergrowth—everything that scurried or hopped or fluttered—streamed along the road. Not even the shadow of the Wild Wood looming in the distance could put a crimp in the day, for summer had announced its arrival.

During those moments when the fickle wind turned their way, they could faintly hear the primitive skirling strains of the hurdy-gurdy playing tantalizing snatches of the old songs; songs handed down from animal to animal over untold generations; songs giving thanks for the gifts of a snug burrow, a full larder, a healthy litter, and the return of another summer. They rounded a bend in the path, and there, in the middle of the next meadow, was the Fair in all its glory.

There was a coconut shy, a lucky dip, and a swingboat. There was a squirrel on stilts and a fortune-teller laying out cards, although on closer inspection, it proved to be Mrs. Otter got up in a purple turban and paisley shawl. There were booths with all manner of enticing fripperies and trinkets for the youngsters (for there isn't a young animal alive who can resist the allure of shiny things). There was sponge cake, shortbread, and jam roly-poly. There were ices of many flavors, and lemonade and barley water and ginger beer, and that most sublime of sticky treats, pink spun sugar. There were

delectables aplenty, enough to sicken every small animal there of injudicious appetite.[9] In the midst of the hubbub stood the Maypole, a tall, stripped birch trunk dangling long strands of multicolored ribbons, waiting for the dancers to weave their patterns around it.

The whine of the hurdy-gurdy was soon joined by the high sweet tootling of a recorder and the jaunty thumping of a tambourine—*chack-a-chack!* A company of red squirrels lined up and began the Morris dance, their bright bells all a-jingle and their bold sashes fluttering as they jumped in steps many hundreds of summers old.[10] A gaggle of rabbits muttered behind their paws, just loud enough to be overheard—"pretty poor jumping, if you ask me," "why didn't they ask *us*?" "we *are* the leaping specialists, after all," et cetera—the way chaps who think they've been wrongfully passed over will insist on

---

9. Please forgive the length of this footnote, but many of these terms may be foreign to the American reader, so let me explain: The coconut shy is a carnival game in which you throw wooden balls at a row of coconuts in order to win one. The lucky dip consists of rummaging around up to your elbows in a vat full of sawdust for a small prize, after which your skin itches like mad for the rest of the day. A swingboat is a huge swing that can make several riders queasy simultaneously, often with interesting results. In some uncivilized parts of the world (which we shall not name), jam roly-poly is known as jelly roll. In those same uncivilized parts, spun sugar is known as cotton candy. Oh, I almost forgot, the hurdy-gurdy is an unsatisfactory cross between the accordion and the lute, incorporating the least desirable features of both instruments.

10. Morris dancing consists of two lines of dancers dressed in brightly colored tunics, with ribbons wrapped around their legs, carrying sticks with more ribbons and bells. The main step seems to be simply hopping from one leg to the other. It is a folk custom that has been around for such a long time that people are afraid to point out how extremely silly the dancers look.

generally acting like damp squibs and boring the innocent bystander with their grievances.

"Look, Ratty," remarked the Mole, "there's old Badger. What a surprise him being here, seeing as he hates going out in Society."

"For heaven's sake, Moly, this isn't Society. Society is all about sitting in a stuffy parlor with dull company, putting on ridiculous airs and droning on about nothing very much, and minding your manners, and balancing your teacup on your knees, and worrying about what others will think of a fellow if he should happen to take the last slice of cake. It's simply the most tedious bosh imaginable. But the Fair, the Fair is quite a different matter! Why, just look around you. It's all about celebrating life; it's about the ripening season, the rising sap. *Quite* a different matter altogether."

A family of field mice played crack-the-whip with the youngest mouse at the end, who came loose and rolled to the feet of the Badger. The mouse squeaked in alarm, but Badger merely lifted him by the scruff, swatted the dust from him, and set him on his feet, saying kindly in his common way, "There you are, little fellow. All right?"

"Yes, sir, Mr. Badger, sir," the mouse quaked. Badger drew tuppence from his pocket and put it in the youngster's paw.

"Off you go. And the rest of you mice, you ought to take better care of this little 'un here."

"Yes, Mr. Badger, sir. We will, Mr. Badger, sir," stammered the others, and then, terrified to a mouse, pattered away from the terrible gray Badger as fast as their feet would carry them.

"Hullo, you two," said Badger, espying his friends. "I thought I'd find you here."

"We're all here," replied the Rat. "Even the weasels and stoats have put in an appearance." A clutch of nervous weasels and stoats, aware that they were there on sufferance, and careful of their manners, doffed their caps and bowed low to Mole, Badger, and the Rat—the three great warriors—who, although they did not condescend to speak to their former adversaries, nodded to them in a nice display of *noblesse oblige.*[11]

"But we're not all here," said Mole. "Where's Toad?"

"Probably waiting to make a grand entrance, if I know Toad," grumped Badger. "And I *do* know Toad. Rather better than I'd like."

Sure enough, the words were barely out of Badger's mouth when Toad's balloon hove into view and drew an appreciative murmur from the crowd. The captain leaned over the rim of the basket, perhaps a bit too far, and cried out, "Stand back! I'm going to drop anchor!"

This announcement caused a stampede of animals to all points of the compass, quickly producing a clearing of sufficient size to allow for a safe landing.

"Oh, Toad," cried Mole in alarm, "look out! You're going to f—"

As if on cue, Toad, the most featherbrained, the most headstrong, the most *addlepated* of animals, pitched forward over the side and plunged to the ground, landing with an impressively loud, squashy, thump.

"Toad!" cried his friends, appalled, certain that the animal lying

---

11. French again. It just means being nice to your inferiors.

motionless on the ground before them (the creature formerly known as Mr. Toad) had shuffled off his mortal coil and was no more. To their great relief, a faint moan issued from the prone form.[12]

"Uuurk," groaned Toad.

"He's alive!" cried the Rat.

"Toad lives!" cried the Mole.

"You stupid bloody Toad!" swore the Badger. The Rat and Mole were too worried about their injured friend to remonstrate with Badger over his shockingly bad language. After all, his provocation was beyond measure.

"Give him air!" cried the Rat to the morbid throng pressing closer for a better look. "He needs air."

Badger declared, "What he needs is some common sense knocked into him. P'raps this has done the trick. And look, there goes the balloon. Probably for the best."

"Where am I?" said Toad, slowly sitting up and gathering his wits. "What's happened?"

Said Rat, "Oh, you nincompoop, you fell out of your aircraft and gave us such a fright."

"I did?" giggled Toad. "Why, so I did." To his friends' relief, he

---

12. The author wishes to reassure the reader that no toads were harmed in the making of this book.

sounded much like his old self. (As you're probably aware, toads are generally resilient creatures and tend to bounce back rather well.) He sat up in time to watch his escaping balloon drift away.

Mole braced himself for a scene of grief and dismay, but there was none. "Toad," he said, "what shall we do about your balloon?"

"I s'pose I'll just have to buy a new one," declared Toad. "Bit of a bother, but I can afford it. Should I go with the red this time?"

This frivolous attitude was too much for the Rat. He seized Toad by the collar and shouted, "You heedless beast! What if it comes down and hurts someone? They could get the constable on you, and the bailiffs, and I doubt the judge has forgotten your last brush with the law for stealing a motor-car."

Toad blanched at the memory of his stint in England's dankest, darkest dungeon, brief though it had been. "Oh, Ratty, what'll I do?" He thought for a moment and brightened. "I know, I'll offer a reward for its return. That'll take care of it." He turned to the dispersing crowd and cried, "A pound to whoever brings my balloon back to Toad Hall."[13]

A whole pound! Toad may as well have uttered words of magic, judging by the effect they had on the crowd. A good dozen of the bystanders hied off in the direction of the disappearing balloon,

---

13. The pound referred to here is a unit of money, not a measure of weight.

a sleek hare coursing well out in front, a collection of hedgehogs trundling along mid-pack, and one stolid, deliberate tortoise bringing up the rear.

The friends escorted Toad to the shade of an oak tree and gave him a refreshing glass of ginger beer. After a short rest, he was able to get up and walk about (although his limp was, perhaps, somewhat exaggerated), garnering many solicitous inquiries regarding his physical state. None of this attention did the conceited animal any good at all, being a naturally uppish and inflated sort. The exasperated Badger finally grunted a few short, sharp, well-chosen words, which caused Toad to rapidly deflate, much in the manner of a punctured balloon himself.

They spent a lazy hour rambling about, nibbling on sweetmeats and various dainties, and then the music signaled that it was time for the Maypole dance. Poor Otter, whose thankless job it was to marshal the mob of dancers into some semblance of order, was too busy to speak to his friends and could only wave in their direction in between toots on his whistle and shouts of "You mice, stop that immediately!" and "Voles! Over here, on the double!" The dancers shuffled and chattered and insisted on standing in the wrong place as the members of an excitable throng of animals inevitably do, especially at a fair, and it took Otter a good five minutes to sort them out. Finally, the band struck up the old tune, and off they went, around and around, circling like the wide swirl of water below the weir.

Mole clapped his paws in time, Toad hummed along, and even Badger tapped his foot. But Ratty did none of these things. Instead, he goggled at the dancers, and stared and twitched and shivered as if with ague. His springy whiskers quivered. His fur stood on end. He looked like a rat struck by lightning.

"Ratty," said Mole, "whatever's the matter?"

The Rat gurgled something incomprehensible through a mouthful of licorice allsorts. *Not* the very nicest sight in the world. He pointed a trembling paw in the direction of the Maypole.

"Ratty, speak to me! Badger, help! He's having a fit of some kind." The Mole shook his friend roughly, but the Rat merely flopped about, loose-limbed as a marionette. The Mole clapped his paws in the Rat's face, but he did not blink. The Badger looked at him keenly and thought hard for a moment, then stood behind the transfixed friend and pointed his long, sharp nose in the same direction as the Rat's, examining the world from the hypnotized animal's perspective.

"Badger, what on earth are you doing?" said Mole. "Have you both gone mad?"

Badger surveyed the scene and determined that the Water Rat was staring entranced at one of the dancers. She was a stranger from the Meadow Beyond, a pretty, little water rat with twinkling brown eyes, lustrous fur, neat ears, and a delicate muzzle. She caught sight of the Rat, and looked away.

"Oh, dear," sighed Badger. "It's no use, Mole—he's a goner. It's got him in its grip, I'm afraid, and there's only one cure for it."

"Got him?" cried Mole in alarm. "*Got* him? *What's* got him?"

The Badger replied gravely, "It is called Love."

CHAPTER FIVE

A Life Forever Changed

In which Ratty goes a-courting.
(For those of you who don't like the mushy bits,
cover your eyes until we get to chapter 6.)

The Fair had been over for three days. Toad was suffering no ill effects from his fall, but the Water Rat was a different creature altogether. He had laid eyes on the beauteous Matilda and gone all soggy with love. He went into a decline, took to his bed, and kept Mole scurrying to and fro, cutting the crusts off his toast and fetching him nourishing broths and restorative tonics. Despite these tender ministrations, the Rat lay flushed and feverish under his quilt, and stared at nothing but the ceiling, now and then stirring himself from his dreadful malaise to sigh deep, shuddering sighs.

On the fourth day, the Rat turned his sunken eyes on his worried nurse and whispered, "Good old Moly. Staunch fellow. What a good friend you have been to me. If . . . if anything should happen to me . . . I want you to have my boat."

On hearing this, the Mole grew exceedingly alarmed and sent straightaway for Badger, who arrived a half hour later in very bad spirits, having been awakened from his afternoon lie-down.

"What's all this rot about?" Badger bellowed as he came through the door. "Rat, stir your stumps![14] Out of bed this instant! You're being ridiculous with this carrying on. Look at poor Mole. Worn to a frazzle, and it's all your fault."

"But, Badger," moaned Rat piteously, "I'm not well."

"Of course you're not well," the Badger fumed. "You're lovesick, and there's nothing for it but to put on your best bib and tucker, march on down to the Meadow Beyond, and tell Matilda how you feel."[15]

"*T-t-tell* her?" stammered the Rat, paling. "You mean, actually *speak* to her? Oh, I say, that's . . . that's . . . Oh, no, I couldn't possibly."

"Ratty," said Badger severely, "are you a man or a mouse?"[16]

---

14. American: get a move on.

15. "Bib and tucker" refers to one's best clothes.

16. Badger is speaking metaphorically (see footnote 5).

The Rat mulled this over. "Well, actually, as you know—" But the irate Badger cut him off.

"Oh, bother! Mole, give me a hand." Together they threw back the covers and pounced on the Rat, who, having made a remarkably sudden recovery, grabbed the bedpost and kicked and thrashed mightily against his attendants. They managed to pry him loose, brush his teeth (with great gobs of foam flying about as if from a rabid animal), and dress him in his good suit, all to the accompaniment of the most unspeakable abuse hurled at them by their struggling patient. Finally, panting, they shoved the Rat out the front door and locked it behind him.

They could hear faint shouts. "I'm an invalid, you brutes! You can't do this to me!"

"Goodness," wheezed Mole, dabbing his forehead with his handkerchief. "I never dreamed Ratty had such a strong grip. I suppose it comes from all that rowing. Cup of tea, Badger?"

"Don't mind if I do."

Mole busied himself with the tea tray and pretended not to hear the muffled thuds of an irate creature kicking at the stout oak door. After a good five minutes, the kicks tapered off, and, thankfully, stopped.

"Should we have been so harsh on him?" said Mole.

"Pah!" said Badger. "I've seen it all before. Happens to the best of animals. D'you reckon there's any shortbread left in that tin?"

⸎

The Water Rat, barred from his own threshold and with nothing better to occupy his time, fumed his way through the meadow. He kicked at blameless clods of dirt and stewed in a thick miasma of ill will. That his oldest and dearest friends would treat him so shabbily. Ejecting him from his very own home. From his very own bed. The stupefying nerve! It was a gross outrage. It was . . . it was such a radiant day that the Rat, who was at heart a most congenial fellow, soon found his bad humor evaporating. He plucked a straw and chewed on it as he meandered, for nothing so focuses the mind on the matter at hand as chewing on a straw. And as the slender golden stem worked its magic, the Rat suddenly realized that his friends were right. A powerful, unreasoning force had taken over his brain, his soul, his very being. He was trapped, snared by that oldest of emotions: Love.

There was only one salve, one cure, for a rat caught in such a trap: to seek out the lady Matilda and confess his condition. He would compose a poem in her honor. He would present her with this token of affection, and hope that she would smile with favor upon his words. The Rat's heart spilled over with fervent emotion for his beloved.

When had the world seen such a comely creature? Such glossy fur! Such winsome grace! Had she not been created for him, and he for her? One for the other, just so? It would take all his powers of creativity to do her justice. From his pocket he pulled forth a scrap of paper and a stub of pencil. (Each of his jackets held the same equipment for just such versifying emergencies, for one never knows when the next gust of inspiration will knock one sideways.)

"Let's see," he muttered to himself. "There was a young rat named Matilda. Oh, honestly, Ratty, is that all you can come up with? No, no, the limerick is such a questionable poem, dicey at best.[17] Let's try a sonnet. Hmm. Shall I compare thee to a summer's day? That's an awfully good line, but I think it's been done before. Try something else. Let's see, what rhymes with whiskers?" He cudgeled his brain for a good five minutes before reluctantly admitting, "Oh, hang. Nothing, really."

The Rat's brain was so preoccupied with perfecting his rhyme that he quite forgot his surroundings and reached the Meadow Beyond before he knew it. He was still fretting over a couplet—

> Ba-dum ba-dum, da-dee da-*deeeee* . . .
> And something something something—

---

17. Indeed. Or as they say in America, no kidding.

when he padded around the bend in the River and arrived at Matilda's burrow. The Rat abruptly came to his senses and gulped. It wasn't too late to turn around and scuttle back to the comforts of his own snug bachelor quarters. But then he'd have to face the wrath of Mole and Badger who, for all their fine qualities and steadfast friendship, could be *most* severe when crossed.

Right, then. Faint heart never won fair rat.

He raised a trembling paw to the brass knocker and froze. It suddenly occurred to him that he knew almost nothing about her. What if she didn't like messing about in boats? Egads! What if she didn't like his friends? Horrors! It was all too awful to contemplate. His brain swirled with dizzying thoughts, and he began to turn away.

At that very moment, a breeze rippled through the reeds along the bank, and from them came a faint murmuring song, at first almost inaudible, but gradually growing in volume. A feeling came over the Rat that he knew the song and he knew the singers; that the invisible chorus was made up of his long-gone ancestors, eons of forefathers and foremothers, untold generations of water rats before him, stretching back, back, all the way back to the misty dawn of time. The multitude of voices twined in a chanting roundelay, and the Rat could now make out these words: "You *must*," the voices sang. "You *will*," the voices sang.

The Rat heard their song in wonder, and realized that he was in the grip of an irresistible force, an elemental rhythm that pulsed in his blood. *You must . . . you will. . . .* There was no turning back. He again raised his paw, but before he could knock, the door swung open, and there stood Matilda Rat in all her rodential glory. And although they had not been properly introduced, and although no word had ever passed between them, a feeling of great warmth and light spread throughout his being. He was suffused with the inevitable, the inescapable fact that she was his destiny and that he'd spent his whole life waiting—in truth, all of Nature had been waiting—for this exact moment. He took her paw in his.

He said simply, "I am the Water Rat."

"I am Matilda," she replied in dulcet tones.

And then a voice came from the dark hallway behind her. A deep voice, rough around the edges. "And I am Gunnar, the Norwegian Sea Rat. We're just sitting down to tea. What's the meaning of this interruption?"

Ratty dropped Matilda's paw and gaped at the silhouette looming in the passage.

The voice said irritably, "If you're selling something, go away."

And with these few words, the hand of fate crumpled up the Rat's dream of happiness and cast it aside like an old scrap of

newspaper. Gone were the ancestral voices, drowned out by the surging of the Rat's racing pulse, which thrummed in his ears: "You *fool* . . . you *fool*. . . ."

The Water Rat—a creature who had never retreated in the heat of battle—stammered, "So sorry," then turned tail.

"No, wait!" Matilda cried.

But it was too late. That intrepid creature—he of the stoutest of stout hearts—had cut and run.

⁂

The Mole spent a large part of his time shoring up the disconsolate Rat, murmuring such phrases as, "Buck up, old man, you couldn't have known she had a suitor," and "P'raps it's all for the best, you know," and "I'm sure there'll be another lady rat in your future, every bit as nice as the last one." Mole understood that the Rat was mourning the loss of a different existence, an alternate life, one with another set of rat's toes warming on the hearth next to his and perhaps a litter of baby rats rushing to greet their father when he came home at the end of the day. A life with a wife and children, a family of his own. But all the might-have-beens had vanished. Only the cold comfort of the never-to-bes remained.

So the Mole reminded himself to be understanding, and this was all fine and good, for that is what friends do for their friends.

They stick by them when the going gets rough; they lift up their spirits when they are low; they are a prop and a stay, one to the other. However, Ratty's moping went on for so long that even the kindly Mole grew positively sick of it. And just when the Mole couldn't take it anymore, the Rat woke up early to a glorious sunrise, threw back the covers, stretched, and peered out his window. There he saw, as if for the first time, the morning sun sparkling on the running water. He sniffed the dank, marshy, inviting smells of the shallows. He heard the exultant song of the skylark. All of these things conspired within him to stir a renewed sense of life. He got dressed without prodding and wandered into the kitchen in search of sustenance. There he found the Mole frying rashers of streaky bacon.

"Oh, Moly," he said, "no rat ever had a truer friend. How tiresome I have been, I see that now. But today is a new day, and as of this moment, I am a new rat. Why, look at the calendar; it's the Queen's Birthday! Let us celebrate the day with a picnic. And tonight let us celebrate Her Majesty's Birthday with a feast. And fireworks! And Champagne! We shall raise our glasses high and toast the Queen and empire!"

"Ratty," said the solemn Mole, "I am so glad to have you back." They shook each other's paw and clapped each other on the back and declared their undying friendship. Each turned away for a moment to discreetly wipe away a tear.

Then they plundered the larder and emptied its contents into a large wicker luncheon-basket, and loaded it into the rowboat. They drifted lazily downstream until they found a likely spot, spread out the checkered cloth, and set to work on their provisions. They ate until they thought their skins would burst like overcooked sausages. Ratty, whose appetite had been stunted for many days, acquitted himself like a trencherman.[18] Afterward, drowsy and replete, they dozed in the dappled green-and-gold shade, and diligently digested their luncheon as the sun moved overhead.

The Mole gave silent thanks that his comrade had survived his near brush with Love, for it was the one force the Mole could not compete with, the one force that might take his friend away from him.

And what would a Mole be without his Rat?

---

18. Trencherman: an enthusiastic eater. This comes from the old days before people had proper plates, when they ate off wooden slabs called trenchers. These were also the days when big, shaggy dogs wandered through the banquet hall for people to wipe their hands on, sort of like mobile hand towels.

CHAPTER SIX

Swordplay

In which Toad has a grand adventure in his very own home
and receives an unexpected visitor.

It is a truth universally acknowledged that a toad in possession of a fortune must be in want of adventure. That is to say, a bored toad is a dangerous toad.

This particular bored toad sat alone in the great hall under doctor's orders to stay inside for a full week, nursing a sprained tonsil (he had been singing in the tub when he had inadvisedly reached for a high C on the final chorus of "A Bicycle Built for Two"). He picked dolefully at the threads of his dressing gown. He contemplated his priceless tapestries, his costly furnishings, his oil portraits of stuffy ancestors. He surveyed his many glinting goblets, his gleaming plat-ters, his burnished silver. Toad regarded all of this and sighed. For what was the use of all these *things* if there wasn't a farthing's-worth of action in them?[19]

"Oh, bother, Toady," he spoke aloud. "Face it, you're bored."

After all, was he not an Animal of Action? Who lived for The Life Adventurous? Who thrived on the cut-and-thrust of Hazardous Exploits, whose meat and drink was Plucky Adventure, who laughed in the Face of Danger, who scoffed at The Unknown, who . . . who . . .

"If only I had my balloon back. Now, *there* was adventure. It's too bad no one's found it." He sighed over the loss of his airship and studied the crest above the fireplace: a quartered silver and blue shield, a steering wheel in the first quarter representing his love of Speed, a golden mirror in the fourth quarter representing his love of, well, Self. The symbol of a dashing, daring, valiant toad, a toad of verve and brio. Should a toad such as he not be running with the bulls, feeling the hot breath of danger on his neck? Should he not be breaking trail over the frigid ice to the distant Pole, reduced to boil-ing his boots for tea? (Although, come to think of it, that might be going too far.) Should he not be thundering across the plains in a sea

---

19. A farthing is only one-fourth of a penny, a fairly useless sum.

of buffalo, the reins between his teeth, his bow and arrow drawn, the ground shaking beneath him from the pounding of a million hooves?

Of course he should. That was only right and proper for a toad such as he, a true swashbuckler who could buckle swashes with the best of them. But here he sat in his dressing gown, shut up inside under doctor's orders, staring at his *things*.

"Shame," he sighed. "Shame that the weasels and stoats are all behaving so nicely. If only they'd step out of line, if only they'd play up just a bit, then I'd have a good excuse to pummel 'em! Instead, here I sit under house arrest. Silly old doctor. Silly old Leech.[20] What does he know about a toad's metabolism? Especially a toad such as I, a creature made of superior stuff. Just look at me. I'm fit as a fiddle. Why, fitter! I can thrash any man or beast that comes my way."

He grabbed the long toasting fork from the fireplace and swished it through the air—once, twice, thrice—and with that, the walls of Toad Hall disappeared in a flash and were replaced by a sleek man-o'-war, HMS *Amphibia*, under attack by a brig flying the dreaded skull and crossbones. The Toad stood on the burning deck and, ignoring doctor's orders, shouted at his men to fire the twelve-pounders: "Fire

---

20. *Leech* is an old-fashioned word for "doctor" because, in the bad old days, they applied leeches to their patients to "drain out the bad blood." So the next time you kick up a fuss about going to the doctor, think how much worse it *could* be.

away, lads, fire away! We'll show those blighters what Jack Tar is made of!" The cannons and pistol fire were deafening; the air was thick with smoke. All around him, crewmen quailed and fainted as the pirates landed their grappling hooks and swung through the air into the *Amphibia's* rigging. Flames licked greedily at the mast, and Toad cried out, "Dowse the mainsel! Trim the jabberwock! Hoist the petard!"[21] At that very second, the pirate captain—the Imaginary Fiend— swung aboard, clenching a dagger between his teeth and brandishing a cutlass of glittering steel. Never had the world seen such a Fiend, with a black patch over one eye, an interesting scar seaming his brow, and, most intriguing, a wooden peg leg, which impeded his agility not at all.

"Aaar," snarled the Fiend in tones that would have frozen the marrow of a lesser being. "So it's Admiral Toad, is it? We meet at last. Haar!"

"You scurvy dog!" cried Toad. "I yield to no man, and the Union Jack yields to no flag, least of all the Jolly Roger. I'll have your guts for garters, sir! *En garde!*" He lunged forward and executed a perfect *balestra,* followed by an *attaque au fer,* before he was beaten back by the Fiend's whistling flurry of *coups de taille.*[22]

---

21. Toad is just blathering away here and making things up. If you look up these words, you'll see what I mean.

22. Sorry, I'm sick of it too, but fencing terms are always in French. It's the custom.

"You devil!" Toad shouted. "Your sword shall not taste *this* toad's blood!" He slashed the air furiously with his fork. "Take that, you villain! And that! Zounds, sir, I'll serve you up a meal of cold steel, I will." (He paused for a moment and murmured, "Ooh, that's quite good. I've got to remember that one.") He whirled back into action, a dervish of a toad, and was about to skewer his foe when the Imaginary Fiend's companion, the Imaginary Parrot, appeared from nowhere. Shrieking blood-curdling oaths, it flew straight into Toad's face, causing him to flinch and drop his fork on the deck with a clatter.

"Oh, I say," he said indignantly, "that's most unsporting."

"Gaar," growled the Fiend, "I've got you now. On your knees and beg for mercy. Which I might or might not grant, 'cos I might or might not be in the mood. It all depends."

Stoutly, Toad declared, "Admiral Toad does not beg for mercy, especially from the likes of you. You, sir, are a veritable parasite of the seas. You're nothing better than a . . . a"—here he struggled to come up with the most scathing insult he could think of—"a *tapeworm!*"

The crowd of sailors and pirates, up until that moment engaged in desperate hand-to-hand combat, gasped and froze in place. The guns fell silent. The wind died away. The sudden silence pulsed in Toad's brain. He glanced uneasily at the circle of shocked faces. He looked at the Fiend and saw a tear glinting in his one good eye.

An abashed Toad murmured, "Awfully sorry, old chap. I didn't really mean it. It just slipped out in the heat of battle. Come along, now, you're not really a tapeworm. Why, you're the very best—I mean the *worst*—fiend on the seven seas."

"I am?" sniffed the Fiend.

" 'Course you are. Everybody says so," said Toad soothingly.

"They do?" sniffed the Fiend.

" 'Course they do. Everyone agrees you're the worst, most hideous brigand that ever flew the pirate flag. Now, chin up—there's a good fellow." Toad picked up his fork. "Come on, away we go."

The two saluted each other per regulation and resumed their swordplay. They lunged and parried, leapt and thrust, and the mighty Toad managed to beat the fearsome buccaneer back to the cabin door, from whence, oddly enough, an insistent knocking issued.

"What's that?" cried Toad. "What's that noise?"

It was someone knocking on the door of the great hall, and the Fiend, along with his parrot, the *Amphibia,* and the rest of the British fleet, evaporated in the wink of an eye.

"Drat," said Toad. "Just when I was about to skewer him." He opened the door to a diminutive figure, a tiny toad wearing thick spectacles and a schoolboy's uniform and cap.

"Why, hullo, Humphrey," said Toad in surprise.

"Hullo, Uncle Toad," said the small creature, peering up through his specs.

Toad shook his nephew's paw, saying, "What are you doing here?"

"Mummy sent me. Didn't you get her letter?"

"I've been much too busy with important business to look at the morning's post," said Toad. "Do come in." He caught sight of the many trunks piled behind his nephew and said, "What a lot of luggage, Humphrey. How long are you stopping?"

"Mummy's off to Italy," said Humphrey. "I'm to spend the summer with you."

"She is?" said Toad. "You are? Oh, well then, jolly good. Always glad to have you. Come along inside. Actually, I was just making mincemeat of a Pirate Fiend.[23] There's a Parrot Fiend, too. You're welcome to join me in the fray."

"I don't play pirates anymore, Uncle Toad," said Humphrey. "I've outgrown them."

"Outgrown pirates?" exclaimed Toad in bafflement. "Don't be silly, boy. Nobody outgrows *pirates*."

Humphrey said, "Now I do inventions."

"Inventions, eh? What sort of inventions?"

"All sorts," said Humphrey. "Those trunks are full of things I'm working on. I couldn't just leave them at home." He glanced around nervously and beckoned to Toad to bend down and receive a secret. "Don't tell Mummy," he whispered, "but I'm making some special fireworks for the Queen's Birthday."

"That's nice," said Toad, and patted him on the head.

---

23. Mincemeat: minced meat, or, as it is called in America, hamburger.

"Mummy gets upset if she knows I'm making fireworks."

"Why should she?" said Toad absently. "Perfectly good hobby for a nephew to have."

"It's because of the gunpowder."

"Hmm?" said Toad. "What was that? Thought you said gunpowder. I really must get my hearing checked."

"Yes," said Humphrey, "gunpowder."

"You have *gunpowder*?"

"I do. But it's awfully dangerous stuff, you know."

Toad gazed into the middle distance, eyes agleam. "Oh, my," he breathed. "Gunpowder."

CHAPTER SEVEN

Toad. And Fireworks.

(Need I say more?)

Toad and Humphrey unpacked the trunks and set up a laboratory in Humphrey's room. Toad exclaimed over each intriguing beaker and flask as they pulled them from the straw.

"Oh, my! Oh, my! So *this* is how you make fireworks, with all these odds and ends? How very interesting."

"Please be careful, Uncle," said Humphrey, finally extracting a tightly sealed tin box, labeled in big red letters: CAUTION—BEWARE—GUNPOWDER—EXPLOSIVE—KEEP AWAY FROM FIRE AND FLAME—DO NOT

HANDLE IF YOU DON'T KNOW WHAT YOU'RE DOING—THIS MEANS YOU. (TRULY, IT DOES.)

"Is that it?" whispered Toad. "Is that the stuff?"

"Yes," said Humphrey. "That's the stuff."

Toad said in remote tones, "Is it the same stuff that one uses to build—oh, I don't know, just for an example—a mortar, say? Or a cannon shell?"

"The same stuff. But, Uncle, you must make me a solemn promise that you won't go near it when I'm not here."

"Mmm?" said Toad, as if in a trance, unable to tear his eyes away from the mesmerizing box.

"You do promise, don't you?" Humphrey eyed his uncle with growing concern and tugged at his sleeve to jolt him from his reverie.

"What was that?" said Toad, coming round. "Oh, yes. Absolutely." He placed his paw over his heart and said, "Toad's word is Toad's bond. Gilt-edged, you know. Take it to the bank and all that. Am I not the most *responsible* of animals?"

"Um, well . . . ," began Humphrey, no doubt remembering previous episodes when his uncle had come to grief.

"Am I not the most *reliable* of animals?" huffed Toad.

"Well . . ."

Toad looked hurt. "Humphrey, my boy, you cut me to the quick.

Oh, I admit there might have been a time or two in the distant past when my enthusiasm carried me away the tiniest bit, and perhaps I was not always the most accountable of creatures, but those days are long gone. You see before you a brand-new Toad. A *prudent* Toad. A *trustworthy* Toad. Now, show me how one makes fireworks, there's a good fellow."

A reluctant Humphrey gave his uncle careful instruction, and they set to the delicate craft of pyrotechnics. Naturally, they took all the proper precautions, for one simply doesn't mess about with such a dangerous item without wearing safety apparel, et cetera.[24] And since an open flame is absolutely forbidden around gunpowder, they worked without benefit of lanterns or candles, with only the light shining through the fine Tudor window.

At last, after they had what Humphrey deemed a goodly store of Roman candles, Catherine wheels, and cherry bombs, they went down to afternoon tea on the terrace. Then it was time to check with the butler that everything was ready for the celebration later that evening. Finding all in order, Toad said, "I think I'll just go to my room and put my feet up for a while." He stretched theatrically and patted away a feigned yawn. "My goodness, I am quite fatigued. I

---

24. I'm sorry to report that certain authorities are upset with the author for divulging information about such things, and they prohibit any further—

believe a short nap is in order. It's always good to be refreshed when guests arrive." He giggled nervously and went on. "Yes, that's the ticket. Tee-hee. Humphrey, would you like to go to the boathouse and amuse yourself? Or perhaps we could roust some of the local squirrels for a game of tennis. Wouldn't that be fun? Tee-hee."

Humphrey looked narrowly at his uncle, who merely blinked and gazed at the ceiling with wide, innocent eyes. Just at that moment, the butler announced the arrival of Mole, Ratty, and Otter.

"Ah!" said Toad. "The very chums I'd hoped to see. You remember my nephew, Humphrey. He's simply dotty about lawn tennis but can't find anyone to play. Isn't that right, Humphrey?"

"But I—" began Humphrey.

" 'Course he is. Simply mad for it."

"But I've nev—"

"Now, run along, the lot of you," said Toad. "The gardener will find you some rackets."

Toad pushed them out the door. Then he hurried up the stone stairs, giggling and glancing about to make sure he was not being followed. He closed himself in Humphrey's room and locked the door behind him. There, arrayed in the gloom, just as they'd left them, were all the necessary items to build an array of impressive fireworks: the string fuses, the paper tubes, the tin of powder.

He'd helped Humphrey assemble dozens of them. How hard could it be? Any half-wit could do it. You simply took a dash of this, added a pinch of that, and *voilà!* Your very own rocket!

What a snap. Any half-wit could do it.

But first he needed more light. The mullioned window admitted little of the late afternoon sunshine, and the room was frightfully dim. So dim, really, that it was probably *more* dangerous trying to work without additional light. Toad considered the advice that Humphrey had tried to knock into his head a scant half hour before.

A careful boy, mused Toad, a conscientious boy. Always has his uncle's best interests at heart. But, he went on, if you consider the boy's essential constitution, he's such a nitpicker. Always nattering on about safety. You'd think he doesn't trust me. Me! His very own uncle! That's real cheek, if you think about it. Safety measures are all well and good, of course, but I don't see how a *small* candle could cause any harm. And the work would go so much faster if I could *see* all the explosives lying about.

Toad searched the room for a stub of candle or a lantern, but Humphrey, in a fit of caution, had removed them all.

"No candles," he said. "He did warn me about that. But surely a match, with its tiny flame, would do no harm. Let's see," he said, patting his waistcoat. "Have I got any matches?" He explored his various pockets and came across not only a packet of matches but his silver cigar case. "Isn't it a fact," he ruminated, "that pyrotechnics require a steady hand? Surely the calming influence of a few cigars would only *boost* one's overall safety, would it not?[25] On the other hand, Humphrey says that there are times when one must sacrifice personal comfort for safety. I suppose he's right, which means I should only have *one* cigar to quiet my nerves while working with explosives. I am, after all, an extremely cautious toad."

He took out a cigar and a wooden match, pleased with his own sober forbearance and self-denial. He closed the packet.

"Meticulous safety is what I'm all about. Why, it's practically my middle name. Or"—he giggled—"two of my middle names, if you want to get all technical about it."

He struck the match, which immediately shattered into a handful of splinters. "Drat," he said. He opened up the packet and took out another. He struck the second match, which fizzled damply.

"Oh, bother," he said. "What terrible cut-rate matches. I really must talk to the butler about it. A first-rate Toad such as I deserves first-rate matches. Never mind," he said, striking the last one. "Third time's luck—"

---

25. Cigar smoking is a filthy habit and not to be taken up under any circumstances.

Out on the tennis court, Mole was about to take his second serve, when there was a sudden deafening explosion, a tragic shattering of ancient glass, a sizzling eruption of rainbow-colored light. The animals turned to see the unforgettable sight of an airborne Toad rocketing past them up into the sky, up and up, as if propelled by a celestial tennis racket, rising higher and higher, emitting a hair-raising yell that grew fainter as he rose into the heavens.[26] And then . . . and then . . . Ah, yes, we come—as we must—to the inevitable "and then." Having reached the top of his most impressive arc, Toad, sadly, was compelled to surrender himself to that most insistent of physical laws, the Law of Gravity, which suddenly demanded that he trade his astonishing upward course for an equally astonishing downward course. He began his return to earth, tumbling end over end in a fascinating display of gymnastics, still emitting an unearthly cry that now grew louder as he approached the observers on the lawn below.[27] He narrowly missed the sundial, with the certain maiming and mangling that alighting there would have entailed, and came to earth in the relative safety of the delphinium bed, which, in a stroke of great good fortune, the gardener had mulched the day before. His gaping friends, who had observed this wondrous

---

26. EEEEEEEEEEEEEEEEEYYYYYYYYYYYYYYYOOOOOOOOOOOOOOOOOOOOOOOOOOOOOOwwwwwwwwww

27. EEEEEEEEEEEEEEEEEEEYYYYYYYYYYYYYYOOOOOOOOOOOOOOOOOOOOOOOOOOOOOOWWWWWWWWWW

spectacle frozen in shock, shook off their paralysis and rushed to his aid with cries of alarm, fearing the worst. To their amazement, Toad sat up and looked around him, singed and lightly smoking. Ratty and Mole batted out the glowing embers still clinging to his charred lapels. A disagreeable odor of burnt tweed lingered in the air.

"Oh, Uncle Toad," cried Humphrey, fighting back tears. "You've blown yourself up."

Toad looked at his nephew and friends. Behind them, the servants were setting up a hue and cry and charging about with water buckets to extinguish the fire licking at the priceless tapestries.

"My goodness, what a wild ride!" Toad said. "I must have reached terminal velocity quite quickly. It was positively ballistic!"

"Uncle," said Humphrey in wonder, "are you all right?"

"Never better," remarked Toad cheerily. "Although, come to think of it, I do have something of a headache. Must have hit my head. Humphrey, my boy, you did warn me. You did tell me in the strictest of terms not to trigger a detonation wave in the powder, although it's more than just a simple shock wave, what with explosive combustion and all. But did I heed you? Not a bit! What a muddled old Toad I am! Shall we go in to dinner?"

He toddled off happily enough, leaving the others trailing in his wake, staring with wide eyes. Dinner was briefly delayed while the servants ensured that every last spark had been extinguished. When the butler finally came in to serve, frowsy and dusted with soot, his facial expression was pursed, as if he'd been sucking lemons.

Toad took no notice. He appeared to be absorbed in thought. During the soup course, he said, apropos of nothing, "In any right-angled triangle bounded by three squares, the area of the square whose side is the hypotenuse is equal to the sum of the areas of the squares whose sides are the other two legs. Did you know that, Humphrey?"

Humphrey and the others gaped at him as he blithely spooned up his mock-turtle soup.

"Pardon me, Uncle Toad," stammered Humphrey. "What was that you said?"

"Oh, just a small quote from our friend Pythagoras, the Father of Numbers."[28]

Ratty and Mole and Otter looked at one another in confusion.

During the fish course, Toad stated, "The smallest prime numbers are, as I'm sure you know, two, three, five, seven, and eleven. There is no largest prime number, according to Euclid.[29] I say, this fish is

---

28. Pythagoras was a gentleman who lived in ancient Greece, long before you were born. He was a mathematician who came up with many original ideas about numbers.

29. Euclid was also a gentleman who lived in ancient Greece. Also a mathematician. One wonders if

p'tickly good. Humphrey, do have another piece of fish. It's brain food, you know. And," he added kindly, "although I'm reluctant to say it about any relation of mine, you strike me as a bit slow for your age. So eat up—there's a good boy."

During the meat course, Toad said, "Archimedes was right, as I'm sure you know. The total weight of displaced water in the bath equals the weight of a floating object.[30] What marvelous roast beef! Cook has certainly outdone herself tonight."

During pudding, Toad said, "An object dropped in free fall accelerates at a rate of thirty-two feet per second squared."

By the time the port was passed, Humphrey had regained his powers of speech and was able to say, "Uncle Toad, I fear that you have suffered some kind of injury." He studied his uncle in amazement.

"Nonsense, my boy," said Toad. "Never felt better in my life. Does anyone care to join me in the library to work on Fermat's Last Theorem? That's always such rousing fun. Or perhaps a game of three-dimensional chess? Anyone?"

---

the Greeks had nothing better to do with their time than sit around and dream up mathematical concepts that continue to vex young scholars to this day.

30. Ditto. One bath day, Archimedes lowered himself into the tub and noted that the water level rose correspondingly. He is reported to have yelled, "Eureka!" which means "I've figured it out!" in ancient Greek. He leapt from the tub and ran through the streets to advise the populace. History does not relate whether he paused to put on his dressing gown before doing so.

Mole said, "Toad, are you absolutely sure you're all right?"

Ratty said in concern, "I think he's lost his mind."

Humphrey shouted, "Eureka!³¹ He may in fact have lost his mind, but he's found a much, much better one!" The other animals regarded him, stupefied.

"I believe, Uncle Toad," he went on, "that you are suffering from Poffenbarger's Syndrome, a rare form of genius caused by a sharp blow to the head. Yes, that must be it! You have sudden-onset, trauma-induced massive intelligence. Good heavens!" Humphrey turned excitedly to the others. "I've read about this. There are only three verified cases in all the medical literature. Uncle Toad, this is smashing! Do you mind if I write a paper about you? I could submit it to the *Journal of the Royal Society of Medicine.* Oh, it's going to be the grandest summer ever!"

---

31. Lot of that going around.

CHAPTER EIGHT

Toad the Genius

*In which Toad's enormous brainpower
solves a great mystery of the universe.*

Toad resurrected a large blackboard from the nursery and had it wheeled into the library, where he spent his time pondering life's Great Big Questions (as Humphrey called them).

One morning, while still in his pajamas, Toad solved the thorny chicken-or-egg dilemma which had confounded deep thinkers for centuries. Over luncheon, he irrefutably calculated the number of angels who could dance on the head of a pin. During afternoon tea, he incisively proved the sound of one hand clapping.[32]

---

32. These are some examples of the Great Big Questions, or GBQs. You may wonder why on earth anyone cares about such things. That is, in itself, an excellent question.

The next morning, he memorized the entire works of Shakespeare. That afternoon, he recited all of *Hamlet* by heart for a rapt audience of his friends, playing each of the parts, even poor, mad Ophelia, moving the Mole to tears with his spot-on interpretation of her floating down the river on her back like an otter, singing aquatic laments until the water soaked her brocade skirts and dragged her to a muddy end. That evening, he devised a surefire defense to the counter-Vronsky gambit in chess, which heretofore had been considered unbeatable. Just before bed, he indulged in the soothing mental exercise of memorizing the value of pi to seven hundred decimal places.

There seemed to be no intellectual area in which he did not excel. Humphrey attempted to measure his IQ, but the various tests wouldn't go that high. The best estimate he could come up with was "really, really whopping."

"Is there nothing he cannot do?" mused the Mole as he and the Rat trudged wearily home after another long evening of being assailed with endless lectures on the obscure theories, paradigms, and conjectures tumbling out of Toad's fevered brain.

"Apparently not," yawned the Rat. "There's no doubt that a good deal of sense has been biffed into him, but perhaps too much, if you ask me. I, for one, am getting tired of feeling thick as a brick in his company. Whatever happened to our flannel-brained, boneheaded friend? Toady, of the simplest of simple minds. I do miss him."

"I've asked Humphrey about it on the sly," confessed Mole, "but he isn't sure if this condition, this Puffin thingummy, is permanent or not. The first, er, victim, got so sick of being pestered about it that he ran away to live as a hermit in the Carpathian Mountains. Humphrey doesn't know what happened to the others."

"Probably run out of town by their friends after driving them all batty," said Rat. "Why, even his poetry is better than mine—although I can't bear to admit it—and he isn't half trying! It's just too much."

Mole felt that he ought to reassure his friend on this score, since the Rat's ditties were close to his heart. But in truth, even Mole (who had something of a tin ear when it came to verse) could tell that the Poffenbargered Toad's poetry was of a much higher quality than the Rat's. Being a wise and kind soul, however, Mole made no comment.

Word of Toad's prodigious brainpower spread throughout the land. Letters of invitation from the great universities arrived, begging a visit from the erudite Mr. Toad. Cambridge, Oxford, Yale—how the clamor went up for the learned toad. Bushels of mail came daily, taxing the temper of the local postmouse no end.

Just after sunrise one morning, as Humphrey was rubbing the sleep from his eyes, he glanced out the window to see his uncle standing on the east lawn, holding what appeared to be a stopwatch and a plate of chocolate biscuits, speaking emphatically to a small rodent, an American woodchuck. Humphrey noticed a big pile of sticks between the two. Then the woodchuck, whom Toad had hired as his laboratory assistant for the day, began throwing—or "chucking"—sticks across the lawn as quickly as his tiny arms permitted, while Toad timed him with the stopwatch. The resulting paper, later published in the *Proceedings of the Royal Society of Intense Philosophical Rumination and Exhaustive Cogitation*, was a triumph. Humphrey, wide-eyed with admiration, read the rough manuscript pages as Toad scribbled them at breakfast and slid them down the long dining table:

HOW MUCH WOOD WOULD A WOODCHUCK CHUCK?
HARD DATA AT LAST
By A. Toad, Esq.

Since the dawn of time, the world's deepest thinkers have struggled with the Woodchuck Chucking Dilemma (hereafter, WCD). I intend to settle the question once and for all; namely, can a woodchuck actually chuck wood and, if so, how much? The question calls for a Scientist with a thorough understanding of forestry, aerodynamics, and zoology. Members of the Royal Society, I stand before you as just such a Scientist.

Let us begin by setting one thing straight: not all wood can be chucked. An adult woodchuck, *Marmota monax*, weighs approximately 8 pounds and can hardly be expected to lift an average log, weighing 10 pounds, much less chuck it any significant distance. In addition, the typical *Marmota*, although of sturdy build, has comparatively short arms relative to his torso, making hurling activities that much more difficult. Perhaps this is why the WCD ends with the wistful caveat "*if a woodchuck could chuck wood.*"

Therefore, the first issue is to turn the typical log into smaller segments, i.e., kindling, of a size that the subject can grasp and throw. Once this is accomplished, the next obstacle turns out to be, quite unexpectedly, one of psychological motivation. If you simply ask the rodent to chuck kindling, even politely, you will get nothing but a few cheeky remarks for your trouble. However, offer the greedy blighter as many chocolate biscuits as he can eat, and you will get a markedly different result.

The details of this study are exceedingly complex and unbearably technical. Therefore, to avoid overtaxing the brains of millions of innocent readers, I proceed directly to the results. . . .[33]

Two weeks later, Toad made a surprise announcement at breakfast. "Well, it's all decided," he said, champing his kippers.[34] "Based on my breakthrough *Marmota* paper, Cambridge University has offered me the Lumbago Endowed Chair of Extremely Abstruse Knowledge, a position that has been in existence for five hundred years. I'm to be Professor Toad, the Lumbagian Scholar of Trinity College! When I think of the role of the many great men who have held the chair before me, extending back into the mists of history, a mighty unbroken chain of sheer intellectual power . . . and when I realize that I, Toad, have been called to stand upon the shoulders of these giants, to share in their legacy, or even transcend it (for I am a toad without peer) . . . I'm overcome just thinking about it."

He dabbed his eyes and said to Humphrey, "I've asked Mole and Ratty to keep an eye on you while I'm gone. And, of course, there's

---

33. Unfortunately, copyright law does not allow publication of the complete paper here. You readers of superior intellect and sufficient curiosity will have to track it down at your local library.

34. Smoked and highly salted herring, often part of a hearty English breakfast. In a word, disgusting.

the butler and Cook. And you have your experiments to keep you busy. But, for the moment, the tailor's coming this afternoon to fit me with my cap and gown. The Lumbagian Scholar must have all the proper accoutrements of his office: a mortarboard, an ermine hood, a black gown lined with crimson silk.[35] Quite the dashing rig, if I do say so myself. Most appropriate for a learned scholar of my preeminence."

There followed a week of much busy preparation and packing of bags and trunks, and Ratty managed to talk his friend into taking the train, severely reminding him of the past scrapes he'd found himself in when he'd allowed himself close proximity to motor-cars. Toad—the new, improved, more *sensible* Toad—wisely agreed.

The big day came. The friends assembled at the station under a cloudless sky to bid adieu to Mr. Toad—now Professor Toad—togged out in his new gown, with his mortarboard tipped at a rakish angle. A new pair of tortoiseshell glasses added the final scholarly touch.

There was much fussing over the mountain of baggage, and double-checking of tickets, and triple-checking of tags, all the

---

35. A mortarboard is one of those flat, squarish hats you see at graduation ceremonies. At that time in Cambridge, professors and students wore caps and gowns over their suits as part of their normal daily attire.

anxious dithering details that occupy the traveler while he waits for his train. Toad dispensed shillings to the youngsters in the crowd and pressed half crowns into the paws of the hard-working porters. A gaggle of juvenile stoats (who, for want of something better to do, slouched insolently against the station wall in the way adolescents *will* insist on doing) watched the proceedings, sneering when they thought no one was looking, and muttering rubbishy remarks when they thought no one was listening.

One of them had the audacity to mumble, "Where's your big fat balloon now, Mr. Toad?" Another, egged on by the cheek of his comrade, added the scathing comment, "Yah!"

Fortunately, Toad did not hear these remarks. But the Mole, with his acute sense of hearing, heard them very well. He sent the louts packing with an indignant quiver of his whiskers and the threat of physical correction.

It was time for Professor Toad to bid them farewell and board the train. Hands were solemnly shaken, and shoulders were heartily clapped. More than one lip was noted to tremble during the sincere exchanges of bon voyage and good luck and promises to write weekly.

Toad boarded the train and leaned out his compartment window. "My dear friends," he said, "my *very* dear friends. I shall miss you all most dreadfully, but a higher duty calls, to say nothing of fame and

glory. I'm off to my rendezvous with Destiny! Humphrey, be a good boy and mind your elders."

The guard waved his flag; the locomotive hissed and groaned and chuffed. The steam whistle let loose a silvery shriek, and the train slowly pulled away.

Rat and Mole and Humphrey stood on the platform and waved their handkerchiefs and shouted their good-byes until Toad disappeared around the bend. Then they turned and headed back home, each with that vague feeling of flatness one inevitably feels after waving a friend off on a journey that entails new horizons and novel adventures, leaving one behind in a smaller, staler world.

"Good old Toady," said the Mole, wistfully. "The Riverbank won't be the same without him. True, he could be an annoying toad at times, but he was *our* toad. Now he will be annoying other people. Ah, well."

"I'll miss Uncle Toad," said Humphrey. "Just think, a member of my own family with Poffenbarger's Syndrome. It's too exciting for words."

They spied Badger leaning against the back of the station house, smoking a pipe in the shadows. Apparently he had been there all along.

"Hullo, Badger," said Rat, with some surprise. "Toad just left for Cambridge. Did you see him go?"

Badger nodded gravely and drew on his pipe. "He's probably the stupidest genius that ever lived. And even though it's a mistake for a Riverbanker to go out into the Wide World, Cambridge might be the right place for him. From what I hear, it's just about the only spot in England where the inhabitants are as puffed up as he is. Oh, and there's Oxford, of course."

"Did you ever in your life," mulled the Rat, "think we'd see such an odd event? I'd have bet my own granny's pelt against it." He thought some more. "Five to one."

CHAPTER NINE

The Small, Bedraggled Weasel

In which Humphrey makes a new friend. (Always a good thing.)

The adult supervision of Humphrey was, from time to time, some-what lax, what with his mother in Italy, his uncle in Cambridge, and his temporary guardians messing about in boats. In their defense, Mole and Rat did visit him daily, and invited him over for tea, and joined him in rousing games of croquet and cricket and lawn bowls. The butler and the housekeeper and Cook, of course, checked on him frequently during the day, but were preoccupied by their duties of office. In consequence, there were many hours when Humphrey was left all alone, which he did not mind in the least, for he was by temperament a bookish child, and the child who is at home in the world of books never lacks for companionship, entertainment, or adventure.

For a while, he busied himself with the matter of replacing all the equipment that had been pulverized in the blast. He spent many long, satisfying hours poring over catalogs and ordering exotic pieces of glassware and other paraphernalia. He also ordered questionable chemicals and certain interesting substances which perhaps, strictly speaking, a toad of his tender years should not have had access to. However, in his favor, it must be said that he strictly observed all protocols for safe handling (unlike *some* creatures we could name).

One lazy afternoon, Humphrey wandered down to the kitchen to beg some baking soda from Cook for one of his experiments.[36] There he arrived unexpectedly in the middle of a violent scene. The butler, the cook, and the scullery mouse had cornered a small, bedraggled weasel who was crying so piteously and profusely that the fur down his front was all soaked through.[37]

---

36. Baking soda is enormously useful in causing things to spew foam in amusing ways. For example, it is one of the essential ingredients in building a working model of a volcano. (But be sure to check with an adult first.)

37. You may remember this small, bedraggled weasel from the first book. After the Battle of Toad Hall, he volunteered to deliver the invitations for the banquet that followed, which makes him a decent sort. For a weasel.

Cook, a large, round hedgehog, spluttered, "We caught him pinching apples in the orchard, Master Humphrey, all red-handed.[38] The very idear!" She turned to the cowering creature. "Why, I've a good mind to turn you over to the law, you rotten little sneak thief." And with this, she drew back her meaty paw and delivered a good clout to the small, bedraggled weasel's ear.

He wailed, "I-I-I'm sorry. Me mam sent me to pick up the windfalls so she could bake an apple tart for me brother's birthday. I didn't mean no harm. It's just that it's Jimmy's birthday and all, and there's no money for a proper birthday cake, so me mam sent me for the windfalls. She said not to take nuffing from the trees, and I didn't. It was only the old mealy ones off the ground. Please, missus, I'm so sorry," he sobbed.

"You're nothing but a sneak thief. The very idear," said Cook, who seemed to have a limited vocabulary for describing dastardly deeds. She aimed another cuff at the cowering creature. Humphrey, who had never in his life suffered the lack of a birthday cake, was moved by the plight of the evildoer, who was guilty, after all, of only the most trivial of misdemeanors.

"Cook," said Humphrey, "do you use the windfalls for anything?"

---

38. Pinching: stealing.

"What?" said Cook. "What's that, Master Humphrey?"

"Do you use the windfalls in making your tarts?"

"I most certainly do not. None of that wormy old muck for the likes of you gentlemen. The groom feeds 'em to the horses."

The weasel, who really was pitifully small and thoroughly bedraggled, looked at Humphrey in mute appeal.

Humphrey said, "Perhaps we could allow him a few apples for his brother's birthday tart. Couldn't we do that?"

"It's Professor Toad's property," huffed Cook. "It's the principle of the thing. The very idear."

"I think that in this case we could overlook such a minor transgression, don't you agree?" said Humphrey. "Just this once."

"Well," said Cook, "I never."

Humphrey plucked a basket from the counter and said to the weasel, "Come along, you. Let's get your brother some apples, shall we?" He unlatched the door and went out through the kitchen garden, the weasel tripping hard on his heels, making stuttering pronouncements of apology and gratitude.

"Oh, Master Humphrey," he said, "I'm ever so grateful."

Humphrey looked at the weasel, who, despite his diminutive build, appeared to be about his own age. "Look here," said Humphrey, "let's not have any of that young master stuff. You can call me Humphrey. What's your name?" And he proffered a paw in friendship.

"Sammy, sir."

"And no sirring, either."

"Yes, s— Yes, Humphrey." They shook paws and made their way to the orchard.

"Rightio," said Humphrey. He examined the unappealing condition of the apples on the ground and said, "I think your brother deserves better than these. It's not every day one celebrates one's— How old did you say he's turning?"

"Six, Humphrey."

"Six, then. It's not every day one turns six. It's a very important birthday. Let's get him some proper ones off the tree, shall we?"

Together they filled up the basket with the finest specimens picked from the branches. Sammy staggered off with his laden basket, enough for several tarts, calling out many pledges of gratitude and friendship over his shoulder as he tottered away.

Later that evening the basket was returned to the kitchen door. It contained a warm apple tart wrapped in a tea towel, the fruit delicately scented with cinnamon, the crust a perfect golden brown. Even Cook had to admit it was a paragon of the baker's art.[39]

---

39. Don't be lazy, you can look this one up yourself. Go on. The rest of us don't mind waiting for you.

༼ ∾⟆◦⟆∽ ༽

The following day, Humphrey and Sammy spent a jovial hour building a kite out of newspaper and lengths of balsa wood and flour-and-
water paste, which stuck dreadfully to Sammy's fur.[40] In consequence,
Humphrey ended up doing most of the pasting. But then, when it was
time to launch the kite, Sammy (who was by far the better runner)
did the honors and bolted across the croquet lawn towing the kite
behind him. After several exhausting sprints, the wind finally
caught it and chucked it higher and higher as if amusing itself. The

40. Nothing distresses weasels quite as much as sticky fur; it drives them quite around the bend.

kite waggled its tail and tugged thrillingly on its long string like a living thing. They took turns flying it until the wind decided it had enjoyed enough of a frolic with them and departed for other chums and other kites.

By then it was time for afternoon tea, which they took on the terrace.

Sammy eyed the biscuits.[41] Humphrey noted this and said, "Dig in, Sammy. No need to hold back. There's plenty." They ate and drank their fill, if not a bit more, then lay back in their wicker chairs and stuporously observed the dumpling clouds overhead.

After a while, Humphrey sighed happily and said, "There is nothing so grand as messing about with kites. Unless, of course, one could actually fly. It's such a shame about my uncle's balloon. He had a big yellow balloon, you know, but it escaped before I had a chance to try it out. I bet I could make it fly again. That's if it's ever found."

"But it *is* found," said Sammy. "I've seen it."

"What?" said Humphrey, with a jolt. "You've seen it? Is it all right? It's not all smashed up, is it?"

"There's a hole in the basket," said Sammy. "One side of it's all shoved in. And there's lots of rips in the balloon that's got to be mended."

---

41. Biscuits: cookies. To further confuse the issue, what Americans refer to as biscuits are actually more like scones.

Humphrey said, "Why don't you bring it in and claim the reward? It's a whole pound, you know."

"I did try," admitted Sammy, "but I couldn't lift it. It's far too heavy for me to carry on me own."

Humphrey pondered this for a moment and said with mounting excitement, "Perhaps if I borrowed a wheelbarrow from the gardener, you and I could retrieve it together and split the reward. What d'you say, Sammy? Would that be fair?"

"Oooh, yes, immensely fair, Humphrey."

And although Humphrey was not by nature a greedy young toad, his eyes lit up at the thought of all the fascinating scientific equipment he could buy with half a pound. There was also the thought of the glory entailed in resurrecting his uncle's expensive lighter-than-air craft, and the opportunity to work on a project that would hone his engineering skills.

"By the way," said Humphrey, "where is it? Is it far?"

Came the reply: "It's in the middle of the Wild Wood."

CHAPTER TEN

Toad in His Element

*Life at Cambridge, where Professor Toad tackles the Greatest
of the Great Big Questions.*

Meanwhile, Professor Toad was making quite the splash at Cambridge. He dined nightly at High Table with elderly Deans and fusty Provosts and all manner of starchy, distinguished scholars. Everywhere he walked, the undergraduates pointed and whispered admiringly: Professor Toad can hear any musical composition played once, and then reproduce it perfectly on the piano. Professor Toad completes the *Sunday Times* crossword puzzle without mistakes in under three minutes. In pen. No! In pen? Good heavens! Professor Toad knows all the parts in the Gilbert and Sullivan repertoire and sings them for amusement in the bath. Is there simply no end to the man's accomplishments? Such a towering intellect! Such a magnificent brain! (Not the most attractive of men, to be sure. A good thing he's so sublimely talented, for he does bear an unhappy resemblance to, well, a toad. Most unfortunate. Especially in light of his name. But we're frightfully lucky to have him!)

On this particular evening, Toad grazed and sluiced sumptuously with the Master of Trinity College, seated under the medieval portrait of the college founder, Henry VIII (who, coincidentally, bore no small resemblance to a toad himself). Following dinner, they took their ease in the Senior Commons Room and drank their coffee and fifty-year-old port while Toad treated the Master to a discussion of his next scientific publication, "Jam Side Down: A Discourse on the Physics of Falling Toast."

"I've always been fascinated," said Toad, "with the jam-side-down conundrum, and now, thanks to the endowed chair, I finally have the resources to devote to this pressing question."

"So, it's true," whispered the Master, his eyes shining with unbounded admiration. "I heard the rumors, Professor, but I hardly dared to hope you would address this thorny problem. I applaud you, sir! How will you attack it?"

Toad puffed happily on his cigar and gassed away. "One could approach it experimentally by flipping a thousand pieces of jam-bearing toast off the counter, but that would be terribly tedious. To say nothing of sticky and a criminal waste of perfectly good toast. No, no, I shall *think* the problem into submission, using Feral Pangolin Quadratical Equations. As you know, Master, my cranial capacity is most astonishing, and once I have solved this trifling puzzle, I plan to tackle a few other matters. Got to keep the old gray matter ticking over, eh?"

"By gad, sir," breathed the Master with a rapt expression, "it's all I can do to keep up."

"Perfectly understandable," said Toad. He glanced around the room at the dozing bewhiskered dons and murmured, "I haven't announced it yet, but I plan to answer the Greatest Big Question of all, namely, Why Did the Chicken Cross the Road?"

"No!" gasped the Master. "Not the chicken crossing the road! Good heavens, man, do you know how many great minds have been derailed by that damnable inquiry? Why, just last year, we lost Professor Armentrout to it, and the poor man hasn't been the same since. Lost all powers of speech, he did. I beg of you, be careful."

"Yes, yes," said Toad, blithely waving away the Master's alarm.

"But I possess the supple intellect and steely resolve the question requires, making me the perfect candidate to answer it."

"Professor Toad," said the Master, "a mind like yours comes along once in a century. We are privileged and proud, sir—*proud*—to have you among our humble band."

There was silence. Professor Toad had glazed over, a sign that he was thinking the deepest of very deep thoughts. The Master sat motionless, hardly daring to breathe. He studied the great man, who was as homely as a potato at the bottom of the bin.

"Hmm," said Toad. "How odd that so many of the Great Big Questions involve chickens. I wonder why that is." He paused and then said, "Oh, look. I've just come up with another GBQ. Have to add that one to the list."

The Master appeared to be a man engaged in a mighty internal struggle. Finally he spoke in low, humble tones. "I hope you'll forgive me, Professor, but would it be too presumptuous of me to ask to *see* the list? That is," he hurried on, "if you wouldn't consider it an invasion of your privacy."

Toad extracted a black leather notebook from the folds of his gown and magnanimously handed it to the Master, who opened it with trembling hands and read the list.

GREAT BIG QUESTIONS
TO BE ANSWERED
BY THURSDAY

1. Why is the sky blue? Instead of, say, a nice orangey brown?

2. What killed off the dinosaurs? Did they do themselves in out of boredom?

3. And why does breakfast *always come before lunch*?

The Master went all swimmy in the head at the last one and passed his hand over his eyes. So extremely abstruse was the issue (and yet such a fundamental part of the fabric of our universe) that he doubted anyone had ever thought to *pose* the question, let alone *answer* it. "Oh, Professor Toad," he quailed, "do be careful. You're pushing the absolute limits here!"

"Worry not, old fellow," said Toad airily, for his grandiosity knew no bounds. "There isn't a Great Big Question that's got the better of me yet. I can wrestle each of 'em to the ground with one paw tied behind my back."

The Master laughed like an enthusiastic hyena. "One *paw.* Oh, I say, that's priceless." A pair of geriatric academicians slumped in postprandial torpor by the fireplace woke to the sound and har-rumphed. Upon realizing they were harrumphing at Professor Toad's party, their scowls melted into weak, servile smiles.

Toad glanced at his pocketwatch and said, "I must be going, or I'll be late for dress rehearsal. The amateur theatrical group is putting on *HMS Pinafore*, and we open on Saturday."

The Master said, "You're playing one of the leads, Professor?"

"No, no. Just a member of the chorus," said Toad, removing his glasses and polishing them with the fat end of his tie. The Master shuddered, for the man's resemblance to a toad was multiplied a hundredfold by the simple removal of his spectacles.

Toad returned his glasses to their rightful perch on his nose, although, as the Master noted, it wasn't so much a nose as a . . . as a . . . well, what exactly was the right word for it? As Toad took his leave and toddled off, the Master, oblivious to the soft snores of the elderly dons around him, remained by the fire. He mused about the great man's unfortunate resemblance to a toad and how Mother Nature, who had so generously bestowed her intellectual gifts on the one hand, had been so cruelly parsimonious on the other when it came to doling out the physical charms.

Two days later, the Master rushed up the stone staircase to Toad's study and burst into the inner sanctum. "Professor Toad," he gasped, "do forgive this thoughtless intrusion. I wouldn't disturb you except that the news is so important. The gentlemen at Oxford (and I use the term loosely, for we're talking about Oxford, after all) are claiming they've come up with something called Artificial Intelligence."

"Indeed," said Toad with narrowed eyes. "And what, pray tell, do they do with this so-called Artificial Intelligence?"

"Somehow they've put it into a device. A device that thinks," puffed the Master.

"Ridiculous," scoffed Toad. "There's no such thing. Next they'll say they've got a perpetual motion machine. I've debunked a dozen of those. They always turn out to be powered by some tiny animal running on a wheel in the bottom of the box. Charlatans, all of 'em."

"No, no," said the Master. "They say that the machine can take one plus one and actually come up with two. Can it be possible?"

Toad mulled this over and said, "Hmm, you're sure it's not just some kind of glorified abacus?"

"My spies—er, research assistants—say not."

"And does this contraption have a name?"

"They call it a computator."

"Computator? Quite absurd. I'm sure there's no future in it, none at all. Now don't fret yourself, Master. I'll come up with something better, you wait and see. We can't have Oxford pulling away from us on any front, not even one as patently useless as this. I suggest you go home and have a good, strong cup of tea. I'll have something ready for you by morning. By the way, if you're going by Magdalene College, tell 'em to send me a dozen earls and viscounts right away. Dukes, if they've got 'em. I'll need them for my research."

Mystified, the Master complied, and soon Toad's chambers were crammed with guffawing young members of the peerage, quaffing Champagne and pelting one another with bread rolls.

The next morning, the porter knocked on the Master's door, bearing an original research paper written by Prof. A. Toad. The Master read it with shaking hands and, overwhelmed, sank into his chair, weeping with gratitude. For Professor Toad had done it again. He'd put those Oxford men in the shade with his magnum opus, entitled "Artificial Stupidity: How to Make It, and Can It Ever Replace Natural Stupidity?"

CHAPTER ELEVEN

Discord and Mutiny

In which our heroes hear rumblings,
and Professor Toad reveals another of his innumerable talents.

The ripening season unfurled at a stately pace. Ratty and Mole spent their days in a leisurely round of boating and swimming and basking in the sun. In the evenings, Mole frequently indulged in the solitary pleasure of a good book while the Rat alternately wrote poetry and chewed his pencil (doing, truth be told, rather more chewing than writing).

This particular afternoon, the pair was relaxing in the Rat's burrow over a game of Snakes and Ladders when there came a ponderous knock at the door. The Mole started, annoyed, and said,

"Goodness! Who could that be?" He had been just about to move his piece up the longest ladder on the board and give the Rat a good trouncing.

Ratty said, "That sounds like Badger. No one thumps on the door like old Badger." He shuffled off to the door where, sure enough, the Badger waited.

"Hullo, you two," Badger said, sitting down in the remaining easy chair. He looked gravely at the Mole and Rat in turn. "I suppose you haven't heard the news?"

"What news?" said Ratty.

"The stoats and weasels," said Badger. "There's some rumblings about."

"Oh, dear," said Mole. "Rumblings of what, precisely?" He was a trifle nervous, for even though he had acquitted himself manfully at the Battle of Toad Hall, and had brandished his stick with the best of them, and had thrashed a great many weasels and pummeled any number of stoats, it was a subject of conversation any sensible, peaceful animal (such as a mole) preferred to avoid.

"Rumblings is only rumblings," said Badger in his common, straightforward way. "That's the trouble with 'em. A word here and a whisper there. You've not heard anything at all?"

"Not a smidge," said Ratty, pouring him a cup of tea. "But surely you can't be serious," he said, then, seeing the look on Badger's face, quickly amended himself. "*They* can't be serious. After that hiding we gave them, I'm surprised they have the nerve to show themselves in public."

Badger went on. "One of the hedgerow rabbits told me he'd overheard a conversation between the Chief Weasel and the Under-Stoat. Said the Under-Stoat was egging the Chief on, telling him he ought to retake Toad Hall now that Toad's gone off to Cambridge. You saw what happened the last time he left."

Ratty said, "But, Badger, you *know* how dim and undependable rabbits are, always getting things muddled up. I wouldn't trust a one of them with my shopping list."

"That may be so," said Badger, "but even the dimmest creature gets things right from time to time. We can't afford to ignore it, 'specially now that Toad's gone."

They stared pensively at the hearth and sipped their tea, each lost in his memories of the terrible Battle of Toad Hall.

Finally, Badger broke the silence. "We've got to send word to Toad. It's time for him to come home."

"Surely that's going too far," protested the Rat. "It's only rumblings, after all."

Badger growled, "It's not just that. You know as well as I do it's not natural for him to be out in the Wide World, gadding about, away from his own kind. Only trouble will come of it."

Rat turned to Mole, saying, "What d'you think, Moly? Should we tell him he's got to come home?"

Mole said cautiously, "Well . . . if it were me, I'd want to know about the rumblings, of course."

They were interrupted by the postmouse at the door, who handed the Rat a thick envelope addressed in a familiar hand.

"Speak of the devil, and up he pops. It's a letter from Toad, and it's addressed to all of us." He read aloud:

Dear Friends,

Sorry to be so lax in my correspondence, but I've been frightfully busy with all my research. Not too busy, however, to indulge in some light extracurricular entertainment. I am enclosing for your enjoyment a clipping from the *Varsity* paper with news of my latest triumph.

I remain, your friend,

Prof. Toad (PhD hon.)

Mystified, Rat extracted a bit of newspaper from the envelope and read the article aloud.

Professor Buttercup?

Crooning Don Wows All in Triple-Hankie Weeper

by
Hiram Satchel

Saturday was the long-awaited opening night of the Gilbert & Sullivan Society's light opera *HMS Pinafore*. But in a dire turn of events, the chanteuse slated to sing the lead of Little Buttercup contracted laryngitis just before curtain. As luck would have it, there was one other cast member who could step in to take her place. But he—yes, *he*—was an untested member of the chorus. I refer to Professor Toad, who, in his spare moments, enjoys memorizing the score to popular operas. Thus, when the curtain rose, the audience was treated to the sight of the multitalented egghead stuffed into a dress and auburn wig, warbling the role of Little Buttercup.

Everyone, including this humble reviewer, predicted disaster. For one thing, the short, stout professor is not noted for his glamour; he bears an unlucky resemblance to his amphibious namesake, which cannot entirely be masked by lipstick and a thick coat of greasepaint.

But I am happy to report that the Professor's impromptu Buttercup was, from first falsetto trill to last, a triumph. Near the end of the second act, wherein Buttercup reveals the dark secret around which the plot turns, there was not a dry eye in the house. "She" was also something of a dramatic dynamo, provoking openmouthed astonishment as she leapt onto the bulwarks of the *Pinafore*, apparently without effort.

See this stunning production without delay. You'll laugh! You'll cry! You'll cheer! And you'll be telling your grandchildren about it ages hence.

The three friends digested this in silence for a moment before the Rat said, "That settles the question, I think. He'll never come home now, not with them all fawning on him like that." The Rat turned over the page and said, "Oh, wait, there's more."

NOTE ADDED IN PRESS: A short verse just submitted to the *Varsity* from some anonymous theater-lover sums it up perfectly:

> *Great actors in greasepaint and limelight*
> *Upon the boards long have troad.*
> *But none can compare with the Buttercup fair*
> *Heart-rendingly rendered by Toad.*

Mole said doubtfully, "There's something about that ditty. It sounds as if . . . but surely not. Do you think . . . ?"

"Penned by Toad, of course," grumped Badger. "That pompous, self-important animal. You're right, Ratty. He won't come back, but I'll send him a letter anyway. We wouldn't be doing our duty as friends if we didn't at least try to warn him."

Badger stood and stretched and announced that it was time for him to be off. "And remember," he admonished them at the door, "keep a sharp lookout."

Ratty and Mole waved him good-bye and returned to their comfy chairs.

"Oh, dear," muttered Mole. He thought about the insolent behavior of the gang of delinquent stoats at the train station. He'd chalked their cutting up to mere rudeness, but what if their loutish behavior had actually been a harbinger of something more ominous?

Ratty spoke reassuringly. "Buck up, old thing. We gave that lot such a tanning last year that they couldn't sit down for months. They'd never have the nerve to try it again. More tea?"

That night, Mole lay in his bunk and tried hard to will himself asleep, which, as we all know, almost never works. He got up and silently padded to the kitchen in his dressing gown and prepared himself a cup of warm milk. He returned to bed with an uneasy heart, and tossed and turned in his sheets for a good long while. When he finally did fall asleep, the susurrant murmur of the River gradually evolved into a voice that whispered in his troubled brain, "Stoats . . . weasels . . . stoats and weasels. . . ."

CHAPTER TWELVE

Swimming Lessons

In which it is proved that not everyone loves the water
as much as a Water Rat does.

"Humphrey, old chum," pronounced Ratty, interrupting the boy as he tinkered with his design for an aerodynamically improved kite tail. "Mole and I are going to take you out on the River and introduce you to the splendors of the Riverbank."

"But, sir," said Humphrey, "I don't know how to swim."

The Rat goggled at him. "You don't know how to swim? Heavens above, what a frightful gap in your education. We must fix that right away. Why, even Mole, the most landlubbered of creatures, knows how to swim. I taught him myself, you know, and now he's a regular duck."

"But, sir, I'd rather—"

"Now, now, Humphrey. No need to thank me. Come along. Moly's waiting for us at the boathouse. Your uncle has all sorts of watercraft left over from his boating phase. Do you remember the boating phase? It came just before the caravan phase, which came right before the motor-car phase, which turned out to be (up until bal-looning, that is) the most disastrous phase of all."

"In what way, sir?" asked Humphrey, reluctantly abandoning his work.

"D'you mean to say you don't know? That your own relation was sent to gaol for nicking a motor-car?[42] Sentenced to twenty years he was, in the darkest, dankest dungeon in the land, from which no man had ever escaped."

"My own uncle, a gaol-bird?" said Humphrey, perking up. "How absolutely ripping! It just goes to show that appearances can be deceiving. I can't wait to tell my friends at school."

"It gets even better," said Ratty. "He escaped."

---

42. Nicking: slang for stealing. And *gaol* is pronounced "jail," despite the way it's spelled.

"*Escaped?*" said Humphrey. "Gosh, I can't believe it! Why hasn't Mummy ever told me?"

Ratty replied drily, "I doubt that any of your relations much feel like talking about it. An escape plan was put in place and eventually succeeded, despite Toad's strenuous efforts to wreck it at every turn. You *could* say he escaped in *spite* of himself. Of course, that's not the way Toady tells it. Ho, no, you'll get quite a different version from his nibs."[43]

"I'm going to ask him about it in my next letter," said Humphrey. "He's sending me some fascinating books: botany, chemistry, physiology, all manner of interesting things."

"That's good of him," said the Rat. "But you've been spending far too much time with your books of late. Why, just look at you, Humphrey, all pale and wan. We need to get you out in the sunshine, put some color in your cheeks, start you on a program of physical improvement. We'll build up your physique with rowing and swimming, and then we'll add some gymnastics. I'm sure you'll be a champion vaulter. Toads generally are. On alternate days, we'll work with the Indian clubs and the medicine ball and, let's see, what else?"

---

43. Derisive slang for a gentleman, or someone who thinks he is.

They chattered their way down to the boathouse, or rather the Rat chattered, expounding upon the details of Humphrey's new program of physical culture. The small toad listened mutely, his heart sinking at the thought of the summer slipping away without his having a crack at finding and repairing Toad's balloon.

"Here we are," said Ratty. Various watercraft were neatly stored in rows, along with every conceivable bit of nautical equipment, all the very best on offer, all shrouded in dust, all with a cheerless and unused air. The Mole was busy pawing through piles of paraphernalia and sneezing.

"Good morning, Mr. Mole," said Humphrey. "Mr. Rat has just been telling me about my uncle's escape from gaol."

"Really, Ratty," said Mole, reprovingly, "the less said about that—*ra-hoo!*—the better. *Ra-hoo!* Now, shall we start with the rowboat today? Or perhaps the scull?"

"Too tippy for a beginner," said Rat, pulling an assortment of oars from the wall and measuring them for size against the tiny toad. "He'll be in the drink before you know it. And he doesn't know how to swim, can you *imagine*? Hand me down one of those cork vests, just for safety's sake."

The Rat secured Humphrey in a cork-and-canvas vest, which was much too big for him, and said, "You'll do. The rowboat to start, I think. Or p'raps the punt.[44] Which do you prefer, Humphrey? We might have to cut these oars down for you."

"Actually," came a faint voice from within the depths of the vest, "if you don't mind, I'd rather—"

"You're absolutely right," said the Rat. "Let's start with the row-boat. Standing in the punt's too much to ask of a novice. Ah, here are some shorter oars."

(The Rat can be forgiven his enthusiasm for boating, since he'd spent his whole life in, on, or near the River. It was both mother and father to him, sister and brother, shelter and sustenance, company and larder.)

It was only a moment's work for the Rat and Mole to prepare the small boat, for they were experienced watermen and models of efficiency. When it was time for Humphrey to get in, he clung tightly to the Mole's arm.

"Sit next to Mole on the cushion and watch me while I row," said Rat. He pushed them out into the River, where the gentle current serenely embraced their craft.

"Now watch, Humphrey. See how you lean forward and catch the water with the oar? Then follow through like this. Try not to splash

---

44. Punt: a small boat used in shallow water. It is propelled by a person standing on a platform at the back and pushing it with a long pole.

too much. It frightens the fish, and they're all a bunch of nervous nellies as it is."

The Rat demonstrated while Humphrey huddled in the stern, one paw grimly fastened on Mole's arm, the other clamped tight to the gunwale.

The party drifted along at a leisurely pace through alternating pools of dappled shade and warm sunshine. The sun sparkled on the rippling water. The breeze bore the ineffable scent of honeysuckle. Meadowlarks trilled their melodious songs. The swifts tumbled in the sky above; the ducks dabbled in the water below. The oarlocks creaked hypnotically as the Rat rowed.

Slowly, gradually, the River began to work its magic on Humphrey. He relaxed his death grip on the Mole (whose limb, truthfully, was going all numb and tingly) and began to look about him. A green leaf eddied by, bearing a smattering of bright red dots which, on closer inspection, turned out to be a party of ladybugs out for the day. A crystalline blue dragonfly hovered above the water; on the bank a passing pheasant saluted them with a shimmering wing.

The Rat sighed deeply, and said, "Ah, yes. There's nothing so wonderful as simply messing about in boats."

Mole said, "There's messing about in balloons, you know, although I've given it up myself. Still . . ."

The Rat soon spied an inlet with a shallow pool that he pronounced a likely spot, and they secured the boat with the painter. Mole propped himself against a tree and opened his new book. It was set on a desert island rather than underground, which was a slight disappointment, but it was nevertheless a gripping yarn of buried treasure and a race to recover it between a daring young lad and a wicked band of pirates.

The Rat lay on the grass on his tummy and commanded his pupil to pay close attention. "Now, Humphrey, concentrate. You move your arms like this"—the Rat demonstrated—"and you kick your legs like this. See? Nothing to it."

Humphrey watched, and shivered.

Then the Rat led his reluctant charge into the water, first up to the ankles, then to the shins, and then to the knees.

"It's—it's a bit chilly," stammered Humphrey. "P'raps we could wait for another day when the water's warmer?"

"You'll soon get used to it," said the oblivious Rat. "I taught your uncle Toad to swim, you know, and he's a regular champion, even if he can't row for toffee.[45] Now, flop forward and start kicking your legs."

---

45. The American version is "can't row for beans."

"But what about my specs?" said Humphrey. "What if I lose them in the water?"

"Oh, bother," said Rat. "I hadn't thought of that. Better give them to me."

Humphrey, who without his specs couldn't distinguish the Rat from the Mole from a tree stump, for that matter, reluctantly handed them over.

"Now, take a deep breath," said the Rat, "and push off."

Humphrey dutifully took a deep breath as instructed, and then . . . nothing. He stood frozen to the spot, the water swirling around his knees.

The Mole happened to glance up from his book at that moment and saw what the Rat in his enthusiasm for all things aquatic could not see, namely, plain stark terror on Humphrey's face. The concerned Mole said, "Ratty, maybe Humphrey doesn't want to learn to swim."

"Nonsense," said Ratty. "He just needs a nudge, that's all." And then the Rat did a thing that some might consider inconsequential and others would consider inexcusable. He gave Humphrey a nudge— just a small one, for encouragement—and Humphrey plunged face-down into the deeper water and, taken by surprise, sucked a fair quantity of the River into his lungs, where it absolutely, positively did not belong.

Oh, the shock and distress poor Humphrey felt at that moment can scarcely be described, to say nothing of the betrayal and anger directed—rightly—at Ratty. Fortunately for all, the cork vest did its job and bore him to the surface, where he spluttered and coughed mightily and bobbed about like, well, a cork.

"Swim, Humphrey," called the Rat. "Do as I showed you. Go on. Move your arms and legs. Go on."

Humphrey turned blindly in the direction of the Rat's voice and tried to flail his way back to shore. The Mole put down his book and stood on the bank. "Ratty," he said in some alarm, "I think he needs our help."

At this point what the Rat *should* have done was pay more attention to the Mole, but being so entirely at home in the water, being so completely at ease there, he could not comprehend another's distress at being dropped into such a welcoming (as he saw it) environment.

The Rat ignored the Mole and yelled, "Humphrey, listen to me. Move your arms and legs the way I showed you. Come on, now—swim."

Poor Humphrey! Blind without his spectacles, deaf to instruction, frightened beyond reason, he churned at the water, actually propelling himself *away* from the bank and farther out toward the main current.

Mole said, "Ratty, I really do think—"

"Don't worry, Moly. He'll soon get used to it. It took you a while, remember?"

The Mole frowned. True, it *had* taken him a while to feel at home in the water, and now he was grateful to his friend for so expanding his horizons.

"Paddle, Humphrey!" cried the Rat, and then muttered in an aside to the Mole, "Whatever is wrong with the boy? I've never in my life seen such an awkward display."

"P'raps we should both get in with him," said Mole, "and—"

"Hulloo, hulloo," came a call from the opposite shore.

"Oh, look," said Ratty. "The otters are out." Otter, Mrs. Otter, and their young son, Portly, were strolling along the far bank and waving.

What happened next took only a second, but note well, a second is all it takes. Rat and Mole waved to their friends, turning their gaze away from Humphrey for the briefest of moments—the time it takes to draw a single breath—and when they turned their attention back to him again, they saw nothing but an empty vest bobbing on the water.

Down sank the toad. Past the darting minnow, past the drowsing newt. Down and down he sank, past the stolid turtle, past the gaping

trout. Cold water flooded his lungs. Black despair flooded his brain. Never before had he known such misery, such hopelessness. Poor little toad! But just as the water began to quench the ember of life within him, powerful paws seized him on both sides and shot him upward to the surface with such force that he broke the water like a leaping salmon. It was the Otter and Rat, grasping him tightly between them. They hustled him to the bank, where the Mole reached down and hauled him ashore like a sodden sack of potatoes.

Humphrey lay motionless, his eyelids tinged an ominous blue.

"We've got to warm him up!" cried Mole. "Put him in the sun! Get the blanket from the boat!"

They dragged him to a sunny spot and spread the blanket over him. The Rat chafed the small toad roughly to stimulate the flow of blood. Then Otter, who'd had experience with this type of situation, propped the small toad up and delivered a series of brisk thumps to his back, causing a remarkable fountain of water to gush forth from the diminutive body. Humphrey gasped and shuddered and opened his eyes. He blinked glassily at the circle of concerned faces looking down at him.

"Thank goodness," sighed Mole. "We thought you were a goner."

"Speak to us, boy," commanded Otter. "Can you speak?"

"My-my-my vest came off," clacked Humphrey.

"My fault, I'm afraid," said a contrite Rat. "Please forgive me, Humphrey. I never should have put you in a vest that size. It was made to fit your uncle, who sports a much, er, wider silhouette. Thank goodness you were only under for a few seconds."

Humphrey, a squashy, pulpy lump of misery, marveled at these words. Surely his ears were clogged with duckweed and he hadn't heard right. He'd been under for a lifetime. Hadn't he?

Rat went on, "Can you possibly forgive me?" He looked so downcast that Humphrey, after a moment's hesitation, nodded. "Thank you, my boy," said Ratty fervently. "Bless you." He turned to Otter and said, "And thank you for your invaluable help."

"Think nothing of it," said Otter, bowing low. "I was glad to be of service. Well, I must be off. The family's a-waiting. We're taking the cub hunting dragonflies." Otter dove into the water and swam with sinuous grace to the far bank, where his family stood watching. They headed on their way, Otter and Mrs. Otter holding Portly's paws between them and swinging him off the ground, their young son giggling and shrieking in delight. What a pretty domestic picture they made! Which was not lost on the Rat, who stared at them with a wistful expression. And the Rat's longing was not lost on the Mole, who felt a resonant pang of sympathy for his friend in his own soft heart.

Mole gathered up the oars and blanket while Ratty retrieved the cork vest. They loaded Humphrey into the boat for the return trip home.

"Never mind, old chap," said Rat, stowing the gear. "I'm sure you'll do better next time, and—"

Mole interrupted, "Ratty, I don't think—"

The Rat went on. "We'll do something about that vest, and I promise we'll keep a closer eye on you tomorrow."

"T-tomorrow?" croaked Humphrey in disbelief.

Ah. *Tomorrow.* Such a simple word taken on its face. Such an innocent word, really. Yet how Humphrey's spirits plummeted upon hearing it, for it was now heavily laden with portentous meaning.

Should Ratty have foreseen the effect of this one simple word on his young charge? Perhaps. Probably. It's hard to say. But when tomorrow came, as it inevitably does, Humphrey was gone. Gone from his bed, gone from his room, gone from Toad Hall.

CHAPTER THIRTEEN

The Wild Wood

*In which Humphrey and Sammy have an
adventure that changes them forever.*

Courage comes in many forms. For a smallish, defenseless toad, Humphrey evinced courage at the moment he and Sammy stepped into the Wild Wood. Of course, Humphrey knew better than to go there, but Sammy, who knew all the trails and passages and shortcuts, and whose mother was second cousin to the Chief Weasel, assured him that they would be safe together. So Humphrey stepped into the Wild Wood, pistol-less and cudgel-less, shielded by nothing more than the friendship of a small, bedraggled weasel. Is that not a form of courage? (Or, perhaps, stupidity?[46])

---

46. The author leaves this up to the reader.

Anyone from the Hall who had been up early enough could have traced the path the two left behind in the silvery dew, first to the gardener's shed, and then straight to the Wild Wood. But no one saw them go. And by the time the cry of alarm went up, the sun's warmth had long since erased their tracks.

They took turns pushing the gardener's second-best wheelbarrow and talked of the glory of making the balloon fly again, to say nothing of the rich reward.

Sammy said, "What are you going to do with your half, Humphrey?"

"I'm going to buy a magnifying glass, I think, or a microscope if the funds will stretch that far. How about you, Sammy?"

"I think I'll buy some winter boots for me brother and me to share, and perhaps a big hank of wool for me mam. Me mam knits up a storm.[47] She has to, you see, what with there being so many of us and all."

Humphrey fell silent and contemplated the yawning gap between full-time ownership of a magnifying glass and half-time ownership of a pair of boots. Then and there, he resolved that Sammy should have the entire reward, for he was a good-hearted toad and couldn't bear the thought of his friend going barefoot every other day through

---

47. His mother is a prolific knitter. You do know what prolific means, right?

the long snows of winter. It would be reward enough just to see the balloon soar again.

The sun was above the horizon when they passed a pair of hedgehogs walking to the shops. They gave Humphrey an odd look but said good morning politely enough. Then they passed a rabbit who cast nervous glances about him as he scurried by. This was not as bad a sign as it might have been in some other animal, for the rabbits were nervous at all times, whether there was good cause or not.[48] Then they came upon the baker making her daily rounds, a comely rat with neat ears and silky fur, carrying a large basket filled with fragrant loaves and dainty cakes; she trailed about her the enticing scent of freshly baked bread, more alluring than the costliest perfume.

"Good morning, boys," she said, scrutinizing the odd pair and their wheelbarrow.

"Good morning, miss," they murmured.

She passed them by and then turned around and called after Humphrey. "Young toad," she said with an edge of concern, "does your mother know that you are in the Wild Wood?"

"My mother is in Italy, miss," said Humphrey politely, which was, strictly speaking, true, although it dodged the real question.

---

48. Rabbits just live in that state, poor devils.

"Italy! Good gracious. But who is looking after you?"

Sammy piped up, "It's all right, miss. He's with me."

"That's all well and good," she said, "but you will be out by dark, won't you? I, and others like me, have safe passage by day to sell our wares, but even we do not linger when the sun sets."

Sammy placed his paw on Humphrey's shoulder and said, "He's me friend, miss. I'll see no harm comes to him."

"I am greatly relieved to hear it." She reached into her basket and pulled out two currant scones. "Would you like these? I baked them fresh this morning."

They thanked her politely and sat down to eat them. She went on her way, casting an uneasy glance or two over her shoulder at them.

They marched on and on, deeper and deeper into the wood, the wheelbarrow growing heavier and more ungainly by the hour. The brush grew thicker, and the beech and elm grew taller, until they came to the darkest heart of the forest where the boughs of the ancient oaks met overhead, blocking out the light. The air was cold and dark and still, and the underbrush was damp where the sunlight did not penetrate; Humphrey shivered and wished he was back at the Hall, or had at least worn warmer clothes. He was weary and chilled and then, to top it all off, managed to bark his shins against a tree root.

After a couple of wrong turns and frustrating about-faces, they

finally came to the clearing where Sammy had last seen the balloon. And there it lay, crumpled against a stump. It was a sad sight indeed, a deflated rubbery skin puddled on the ground like a yellow pond. Its many lines were tangled in vicious snarls, and the wicker basket was partly smashed in.

Humphrey's heart sank, for although Sammy had warned him, he hadn't imagined it in such a sorry state. It was no longer noble or glorious; in fact, it was no longer recognizable as an airship. He circled the wreckage, muttering, "Oh, dear, oh, dear, what a shame. Another of Uncle Toad's grand schemes come to grief. Still, we might be able to fix it once we get it home."

"What about the pound?" Sammy said anxiously. "We'll still get the pound, won't we? Even though it's a smash-up?"

"Yes," said Humphrey, "we'll still get the pound. Uncle Toad just wants it back. He didn't say it had to be flyable."

"You're sure?" fretted Sammy, visions of new boots and woolly scarves dancing away just out of reach.

"Oh, yes, most generous is Uncle Toad. He's never mean with his money." He held up a section of the canopy and examined a long rip. "Hmm. I think this piece could be sewn together without too much difficulty. Now, that bit over there . . . that looks like another matter entirely."

So intent was Humphrey on examining the pathetic remains that he did not notice two sharp wedge-shaped faces in the undergrowth, watching his every move with hard, calculating eyes.

"All right," Humphrey said. "I think I've figured it out. We'll have to cut some of these lines, roll the canopy up, put it in the wheelbarrow, and then put the basket on top. Good thing I've got my pocket knife."

They bent to their task, and at that very moment, out from the bushes stepped the Chief Weasel and his hard-boiled henchman, the Under-Stoat.

"Hello, young Sammy," purred the Chief. "Won't you introduce us to your friend?"

Humphrey froze, his knees turned to jelly. His every instinct shrieked at him to flee, to run from there just as fast as his feet would carry him, but his legs would not obey. He stood rooted to the spot in primordial terror.

"Don't be afraid," crooned the Chief in silky insinuating tones. "You're our guest here. We was just about to have us a bite of lunch, and we was so hoping you could join us. Sammy, do the honors and introduce us."

Sammy squirmed uneasily. "Uh, Chief, this is my friend, Humphrey."

"Ah, young Marster Humphrey. Pleased to make your acquaintance, I'm sure." The Chief bowed.

The Under-Stoat sniggered nastily and said, "Yeah, ri'. *Pleased.*"

The Chief Weasel elbowed him and snapped, "Get our lunch, you, and look sharpish about it. I'm sure these young gentlemen are plenty fatigued from their long walk. And mind you don't forget the table-cloth." The Under-Stoat slunk into the brush and returned a moment later with a checkered cloth and a basket that he proceeded to unpack.

Humphrey found his voice and squeaked, "That's—that's most kind of you, sir, but I'm expected back at Toad Hall."

"Is that right?" said the Chief Weasel in a casual sort of way. "Last I heard, your uncle was off at Cambridge. Here, come and sit down. There's all sorts of good things to eat."

Humphrey glanced tensely at Sammy, whose eyes were fastened on the meat pies and sausage rolls being spread before them, and said, "Don't you think it's time to go?"

Sammy said eagerly, "Let's stay for a bite, Humphrey. That currant scone was an awful long time ago." He plunked himself down.

Humphrey hesitated. His stomach agreed that the currant scone had indeed been an awfully long time ago. And although the stoat and weasel standing before him were the very ones he'd been warned about, they smiled warmly and exhibited concern that he feel at home. Sammy's mother was second cousin to the Chief Weasel, was she not? And wouldn't it be sheer rudeness to leave at that point? The food lay before him. His stomach cast the decisive vote by grumbling loudly. He sat down.

"Tuck in, you two."[49] The Chief smiled. He proved to be surprisingly good company, making engaging small talk and inquiring

---

49. American: dig in.

kindly about the Mole and the Rat and Mr. Badger and Professor Toad, and were they in good health, and how were they spending their time, and who was going on holiday, and exactly where and when. He also expressed great interest in the principles of lighter-than-air flight, asking many questions about how the balloon might possibly be fixed, and if Humphrey thought it could ever fly again.

Finally, when all had eaten their fill, Humphrey brushed the last crumbs from his lap and said, "Mr. Chief Weasel, thank you so much for lunch. But it's time for us to be heading back. If you don't mind, we'll just load up the balloon and be on our way."

"Ah. Well." The Chief Weasel stroked his whiskers. "It's about the balloon. There is something you can do for us." His expression changed, and he pinioned Humphrey with an evil smile that made the toad's blood run cold. " 'Course, you'll have to stay with us awhile."

CHAPTER FOURTEEN

The End of Professor Toad

*In which Professor Toad is unmasked
in a most violent and unfortunate manner.*

It was one of those long, mauve twilights that magically lingers on, seemingly past its appointed time. The evening star, dallying in the purple wings, peeped out shyly, as if reluctant to nudge the day from the stage. The butterfly loitered on the vine; the bee yet tarried at the rose. A wren in the shrubbery warbled itself hoarse.

It should have been a perfect day. It *had* been a perfect day. Up until this point.

Professor Toad and the Master took a turn at their leisure around the Great Court, the gravel crunching underfoot, the soft air caressing their brows.

"As you know," opined Toad, "Professor Newton was a great man. I'm not saying he was *not*. But I sometimes think his reputation has been a bit, well, *inflated* over the centuries, a bit *burnished,* if you will, by the passage of time. I myself believe . . ." he nattered on, for Toad, who had always loved the sound of his own voice, loved it even more now that he had actual opinions to express to an adoring public. The Master leaned in close (but not too close, for if ever there was a definition of an Englishman as a chinless wonder, Professor Toad was a most unlucky example) and breathed many encouraging lines such as "Fascinating" and "D'you mean to say—?" and "Do go on."

They were deep in a discussion of Newton's Laws of Motion when the porter ran up brandishing a telegram.

"Professor Toad," he said, "I'm sorry to interrupt you, sir, but there's a telegram marked 'urgent' for you."

"Thank you, my good man," said Toad. He opened it while the Master tactfully looked away and hummed to himself to afford the great man some degree of privacy.

"Oh, dear!" exclaimed Toad.

"Not bad news, I hope?" inquired the Master with concern.

"It's a message from Toad Hall. It seems that my nephew,

Humphrey, has disappeared. Dashed strange, this. It's not like him to just wander off. He's a good boy, a responsible boy."

"You must go at once," said the Master. "There's still time to catch the last train."

"Of course, of course," agreed Professor Toad. "But what about the theoretical astrophysics seminar?"

The pair were so engrossed in their conversation that they wandered, without noticing, into one of those spontaneous games of undergraduate cricket which—although strictly forbidden—break out from time to time like a bad rash.[50] North bowled a fast bowl with top-spin that hurtled wildly off South's bat ("Oh, well played!") straight for the pair of academics. And although the students shouted a warning, and although the professors could have seen the ball coming if they'd been paying attention—alas!—such was not the case, and the cricket ball beaned Professor Toad on the head, knocking him sideways.

Poor Toad! Victim of the same physical laws he had just been discussing.[51] He tumbled onto the grass and rolled several times, as

---

50. Cricket is a sport whose closest American relative is baseball (a third cousin twice removed). It is an ancient game with so many strange and convoluted rules that not even professional umpires understand them all. Entire books have been written trying to explain it. For example, here are some names of team positions: silly mid on, silly mid off, and deep backward square leg. And don't get me started on the "leg before wicket" rule. It's hopeless.

51. When an object (such as a toad) is acted upon by an external force (such as a cricket ball), the velocity of the toad will change in proportion to the force of the ball applied to it.

those of portly build are wont to do. His cap flew in one direction, his glasses in another. The Master, appalled, called out to the students, "Hi, you! Out of here! I'll deal with you lot later." He turned to Toad and said, "Oh, Professor Toad, I am so sor—"

The Master gaped in astonishment at the dazed tubby figure seated before him on the grass, its gown hiked up in a most undignified way, its knobby knees on view for all the world to see.

Toad blinked.

"*You!*" yelled the Master. "Who are you, you horrid little man, and what have you done with Professor Toad?"

"Master," said Toad after a moment, "it's me. That is to say, it is I, Professor Toad. Don't you recognize me? I'll prove it, just listen. The son of the squaw on the hippopotamus hide is equal to the sons of the squaws on the other two hides.[52] Oh, bother," said Toad, perplexed. "That doesn't sound quite right somehow."

The Master bent down. He peered into Toad's face and then recoiled in shock. "Good gracious," he sputtered. "Professor Toad, you're a . . . he's a . . . it's a . . . *toad!*"

"That's true," admitted Toad. "But, you know, I never said I wasn't." He climbed to his feet, retrieved his cap, and swatted blades

---

52. What he *meant* to quote was Pythagoras's Theorem, see page 76. What he *actually* said was the punch line to an extremely old joke, which goes like this: [Oh, sorry. My editor is waving me on.]

of grass from his gown. "Previously Toad of Toad Hall, and now Professor Toad of Trinity College. At your service, sir." He bowed politely. "I say, have you seen my glasses?"

The Master teetered on the edge of apoplexy and turned purple to his hairline. "A nasty . . . crawly . . . vile . . . toad!"

"Hang on, there's no need for that," said Toad, affronted.

"A foul, loathsome, *warty* toad," bellowed the Master.

"A baseless lie!" cried Toad. "For your information, sir, I've never had a wart in my life."

The Master said, "I've long wondered why you don't have a chin, and now it all comes clear to me." He roared after the undergraduates, "Come back, come back here! Come and seize this repellent, revolting, disgusting creature!"

"Oh," whimpered Toad, "surely that's a bit harsh. Why, I was only just—" He looked up to see the clutch of students bearing down on him, their gowns fluttering like black flags of doom.

"I can explain everything!" Toad cried, nevertheless leaping to his feet and dashing off in the opposite direction. "It all started out when I was making fireworks, you see," he called over his shoulder, only to see the wild gang of students gaining on him. The Master, a man of some years, brought up the rear of the pack but was nevertheless exhibiting good form and acquitting himself nicely over the short distance.

"I can explain! Honestly!" wheezed Toad, and then, realizing he needed to save his wind for escape, put his head down and ran grimly at top speed for the Backs and the River Cam.

"Impersonator!" bawled the Master. "Call the porter! Call the police!"

"Charlatan!" bayed the undergraduates. "Stop that toad! Seize him!"

Toad, short of leg and round of torso, ran as he'd never run before. In a wild panic, he inadvertently took the only sensible course left open to him: He vaulted over the railing of the bridge into the River Cam a few feet below, startling the last of the day's punters.

He rose to the surface, hacking and coughing. His pursuers leaned over the bridge, shaking their fists and calling him unprintable names.

"Ha!" he jeered. "You've been outfoxed by the Toad ag—" he had just enough time to shout before his waterlogged gown dragged him under. Wriggling and kicking, he managed to extricate himself from its folds and bobbed to the surface once more. To his dismay, he saw his pursuers running down from the bridge and fanning out along the towpath beside the river, which was, in truth, narrow enough to be described as a mere brook. A mere brook from which an under-graduate with a strong arm and a boat hook could, without even wetting his feet, pluck the most reluctant of toads.

And although Toad dearly wanted to explain his circumstances, and be reinstated into the fold of academia (or at least hurl some choice insults at his tormentors), he realized that sticking around to do so would only bring him a large ration of grief. Taking a deep gulp of air, and pushing off with a powerful frog kick, he swam away down the Cam for all he was worth.

CHAPTER FIFTEEN

Very Bad News

In which our heroes learn of Humphrey's fate.

It was a grim and exhausted trio that convened before the fire in the library of Toad Hall that night, worn and filthy.

"Not a trace," muttered Mole. "Not a jot, not a tittle."[53]

"But that's a good thing," said the downcast Rat. "Isn't it? If he . . . if he were hurt, or . . . or worse . . . we'd have found some kind of sign." The others looked at him in silence. He added uncertainly, "Wouldn't we?"

---

53. You out there, stop that giggling immediately. This means that there was no sign at all, not even a tiny one.

"The thing I don't understand," rumbled Badger, "is why the gardener's second-best wheelbarrow is missing. It's got to mean something, but I can't for the life of me figure it out."

"And why haven't we heard from Toad?" said Mole. "His own flesh-and-blood gone missing, and we haven't heard a word. P'raps we should send him another telegram tomorrow."

They stared in dismal silence at the flickering fire, which crackled and sparked cheerily, oblivious to the heavy gloom that permeated the three friends.

Finally Badger said, "We've done everything we can for today. I propose we all spend the night here and get up early in the morning for a fresh start." The Badger, a creature of habit, loathed spending the night away from the familiar comforts of his own burrow. The other two were well aware of this and rightly interpreted his volunteering to stay as a statement that he was, in fact, worried sick.

"Right," said Rat dispiritedly. "Off to bed it is."

They trudged up the grand staircase to the guest wing. Before turning in, Mole looked in on Humphrey's silent bedroom one last time, as if hoping that the mute objects tidily stacked there, the chemistry set, the many books, even the kite, could somehow reveal their young master's plight.

The next morning found them poorly rested and ill-tempered. They sat in the breakfast room and, despite having no real appetite, forced themselves to down many bowls of thick porridge and cups of sugared tea, fortifying themselves for the long day ahead. There was still no telegram, no letter, no word at all from Toad.

"It's bad enough we have to worry about Humphrey," complained Ratty, "but now we have to worry about Toad as well."

"No, we don't," snapped Badger. "I refuse to worry about that boneheaded animal. Let him worry about himself. We need only concern ourselves with Humphrey."

"But, Badger," protested the Mole, "what more can we do? We've searched everywhere."

Badger fixed his gaze on Mole with a lowered brow. "We have not searched everywhere. We have not searched the Wild Wood."

A millipede of fear skittered down the Mole's spine. He shuddered and said vehemently, "Surely he wouldn't have gone there. He *knows* better."

The Rat said, "Badger's absolutely right. We have to go in. Don't worry, Moly. You and I will stick together. We'll arm ourselves to the teeth, and we'll be sure to get out before dark. That'll be all right, won't it, Badger?"

Badger, who was the only one of them large enough and formidable enough to travel through the Wild Wood alone, nodded gravely.

Rat led them into the weapons room and distributed to each of them a stout cudgel, a pistol, and a thick belt in which to tuck them. Then it was down to the kitchen for a packet of sandwiches and a flask of tea. Just as they were finishing their preparations, a tentative knock sounded on the kitchen door.

"Humphrey!" cried Rat. "He's home!" He leapt to the door and flung it open. But instead of Humphrey, there stood a small, bedraggled weasel.

"What do you want?" said the Rat crossly. "We've no time for you at the moment. Come back another time."

Mole, who had a few days earlier noted the weasel and Humphrey cavorting on the lawn with a kite, said not unkindly, "Come in, come in, but be quick about it."

The weasel quaked with fear at the sight of the armed band, fearsome as any brigands. He said faintly, "P-please, sir. I'm not supposed to be here. You won't tell anyone, will you?"

"Speak up," said the Mole.

"It-it-it's—" stammered the weasel.

"You're Sammy, right? Come along, now. Out with it," said the

Mole, shaking him a bit more roughly than he meant to, for he was a very worried Mole indeed.

The shaking did the trick, loosening the words that had stuck in Sammy's throat. "It's Humphrey, Mr. Mole, sir. He's in the Wild Wood."

"You know that for a fact?" said Badger ominously.

"Oh," Sammy whispered, "I'm not supposed to tell you. There'll be such trouble."

"There'll be real trouble in a minute if you don't tell us what you know," snarled the Badger, advancing on the shivering animal. Sammy, faced with such a dreadful apparition, took the only sensible course of action open to him and fainted clean away. He came around a few minutes later to find the Mole flapping a tea towel in his face.

"There, there," said the Mole soothingly. "Mr. Badger didn't mean to frighten you." He threw a warning glance at the Badger, who sat stolidly at the far end of the kitchen table, where he'd been banished by Mole. "Now, sit up, there's a good boy, drink this, and then tell us everything you know." He thrust a mug of hot milky tea into Sammy's paw and made encouraging noises for him to drink up. After some fortifying sips, and with many a worried glance at Badger, Sammy was able to speak again.

"Humphrey and me made a plan, see," he said. "It's about Mr. Toad's balloon, what come down in the middle of the Wild Wood."

"Oh, dear!" exclaimed Mole, wishing the conversation would take any turn except this one.

Sammy nodded and said, "Yes sir, that's ri'. And Humphrey and me was going to bring it back here and go halvsies in the reward that Mr. Toad put up. Split it down the middle, fair and square. But the balloon's awful big and heavy, so we borrowed a wheelbarrow." He added quickly, "We only borrowed it, you understand. We was going to put it back. But when we finally got to the balloon, there was the Chief Weasel and the Under-Stoat waiting for us."

"Poor Humphrey," exclaimed Rat. "He must have been terrified."

"Not so bad, sir," said Sammy. "They acted all friendly. Said we was their honored guests and all. Then they was asking him all sorts of questions about the balloon and could he make it fly. 'Course he can, I told 'em. My friend Humphrey knows all about balloons and inventions and such," said Sammy proudly. "I told 'em that."

Badger spoke, his voice deadly soft. "You didn't. Did you?"

Sammy went all pale and wobbly.

"Badger," murmured the Mole, "please let me handle this. Go on, Sammy. Don't mind Mr. Badger."

"S-so then they asked him what he might need to fix it. It's the Chief Weasel's birfday coming up, and he mentioned how he wanted to celebrate with a balloon ride. They was acting so nice and polite, and they insisted we stay for lunch, and such a terribly nice lunch it was. And then . . . and then . . . when it was time for us to be getting back . . ." He sniffled.

"Go on," urged the Mole.

Sammy erupted in a sudden fountain of tears. "They said he had to stay! They said he had to fix it. He had to make it fly, or else they'd never let him go!"

CHAPTER SIXTEEN

Toad on the Road

*In which Toad, who must find his way home on limited brainpower,
has a brush with the law.*

Toad dreamt he was back at Toad Hall. He dreamt he was sleeping in his own featherbed, nestled in a snug pocket of fine linen sheets. He dreamt that there *weren't* scratchy bits of hay working their way up his sleeves and down his neck, that he *wasn't* itching all over in the most dreadful way, that the urgent need to sneeze *wasn't* tickling his nose. But as with every other dream, this one had to end. He woke up sneezing and found himself in a haystack. There were indeed bits of hay working their way down his shirt, and he was in fact itching, horribly, all over. "Oh, drat," he groaned, yawning and scratching. "Oh, bother."

He hauled his squat figure down from the stack and tried to shake out his clothes.[54] The night before, climbing into the hay had seemed like such a good idea. Now he knew it for what it was: a terribly bad idea. He scratched himself furiously and looked about in the half-light. The farmer's house in the distance was showing signs of life, and wasn't that a dog he heard, barking to be let out? A huge, slavering beast, no doubt, who breakfasted on toads.

He hurried away across the field.

Noon found the weary Toad trudging along a dusty footpath, the midday sun bearing down upon him like an anvil. Heretofore he had always looked upon the sun as his friend, a delightful companion during the all-too-brief summer months. But now it bludgeoned him with sadistic tropical fury and mocked his tortuous progress homeward. He'd never in his life been so thirsty and hot. What wouldn't he give just now for a small rain cloud, if only one could be ordered up?

---

54. Those of you who've spent the night in a haystack know that this is well nigh impossible. But for those of you who haven't, well, think of the last time you got a haircut and a few of the tiny hairs went down your neck. Then multiply that by, oh, about ten thousand, and you get the general idea.

Why, half his fortune, willingly. He'd never in his life been so hungry and tired. What wouldn't he give for a simple mug of tea and a humble fried egg sandwich? The rest of his fortune, gladly. He came at last to a road and a signpost. To the left lay Retchford and East Retchford; to the right, Wopping Crudworth. Not one of these towns was familiar to him.

"Oh, this is all too much," he cried. He shook his fists at the sun and yelled unprintable curses at it, ordering it to go away. But the sun completely ignored him.[55]

"Why me? Why me?" he yelled.[56] He threw himself to the ground and pounded the hot dust with his fists and kicked his legs and rolled about most disgracefully, all the while weeping petulant tears. None of which did him the slightest bit of good. After a few minutes, he realized he was making a spectacle of himself, and he sat up, covered in powdery dust from head to toe, looking somewhat spectral.

"Think, Toady," he murmured to himself. "Think, think, think."

It would have been nothing for Professor Toad to analyze the situation and extricate himself from it, but it appeared that Professor Toad had departed forever, leaving behind plain old Mr. Toad, who

---

55. The sun is like that.

56. The answer to this question is, of course, "Why *not* you?" Life is simply not fair, and the sooner you get used to it, the easier things will go for you.

had spent his life thinking as sparingly as possible. He applied himself for a moment or two, but the effort was such a strain on his dim brain that it gave him a headache.

"My head hurts, and my feet hurt, and my stomach is growling so loudly I can't hear myself think. But if I *don't* think my way out of this, I will sit here forever and ever. They will find me ages hence, the shriveled remnant of a toad. Oh, it really is too much."

He pondered his dilemma. What would Moly do? What would Ratty do? What would Badger—no, no, he shuddered. Best not to insert oneself into the mind of Badger; no telling what lay there. But Moly and Ratty, his dearest friends, his oldest compatriots, what advice would they give him? Before he realized it, he found himself thinking hard on the question. After a few moments of this, his friends' voices whispered the answer in his head: "You must find the River, Toad. Not just *a* river, but *the* River. Find it, and it will show you the way home."

Toad jumped to his feet, exclaiming, "Of course! That's it! What a clever toad am I. Why, I'll just find the River. . . ." He looked about for a sign pointing the way, but alas, there was none. He frowned and thought some more. He could sit in the road and wait for a passerby, but he might be spotted for a fugitive. He could pick a direction and strike out at random, but he ran the risk of putting more distance between himself and his home. He idly surveyed the stone wall on the other side of the road, over which a tall wooden stile passed.[57] The voice of Ratty in his head urged, "Go on, Toad, climb to the top of the stile."

"But it's hot," Toad whined, "and I'm tired. Why should I exert myself in the heat?"

Mole's voice scolded, "You'll be able to see the countryside from there, that's why, you ninny. Now, stir your stumps."

"Oh, all right," said Toad, ungraciously. He looked first one way down the road, and then the other, as one should always do. Seeing no motor-car or pedestrian, he trotted across and hauled himself up the rickety steps. Puffing, he surveyed the scenery, and what did he see?

"Nothing," he moaned, "not a blasted thing."[58]

That is to say, no River. There were miles of breathtaking land-scape stretching from one horizon to the other, but no River.

"Not a thing," he whimpered. And then . . . and then . . . was there something in the air? Something . . . familiar? The barest hint—more a sense of nostalgia than an actual smell—of something known to him? Toad sniffed tentatively, sampling the points of the

---

57. A stile is a set of stairs over a wall. Farmers use them to cross from one fenced pasture to another.

58. There is simply no excuse for such foul language, even if one *is* completely alone.

compass. If he'd been lucky enough to be born with whiskers, they would have quivered on end.

Yes! There it was again. The merest thread, a filament of scent, vaguely reminiscent of mud and marsh and rich, rank sediment. He sniffed again. Deep within him tingled some sympathetic vibration, some primitive instinct, some ancient sense of home and safety.

Yes! The River! He was sure of it. It was coming from straight ahead, down the hill.

"Oho!" he cried. "I've done it! Home lies that way, I can feel it in my bones. Am I not the cleverest of toads? Why, they were lucky to have me at Cambridge. Am I not the brainiest, the most gifted and talented toad in all the world? And let's not forget handsome. And modest."

And with this and many other disgustingly boastful sentiments, he struck off across the fields with a jaunty gait, quite the restored Toad, puffed up with vanity and conceit, overflowing with braggadocio, his thoughts of hunger and fatigue washed away in a warm bath of self-congratulation, nauseous in degree.

Twice he had to crawl into the hedge to hide from strangers, which took him down a peg or two, but he soon came to a village. The streets were strangely quiet and deserted, and he was able to sidle his way around the houses and shops until he came at last to the post office where, stuck on a pillar for all the world to see, was a picture of a toad's countenance. Printed above it in large letters was the single word WANTED. Printed below it, in equally large letters, was the word FUGITIVE.

Fine print at the bottom read FOR THEFT OF A MOTOR-CAR; FOR RECK-LESS DRIVING; FOR ESCAPE FROM HER MAJESTY'S DUNGEONS BY IMPERSONAT-ING A WASHERWOMAN; FOR GROSS IMPERTINENCE TO THE RURAL POLICE; FOR OTHER MISCELLANEOUS AND SUNDRY EXAMPLES OF UNACCEPTABLE BEHAVIOR TOO NUMEROUS TO MENTION HERE.

Toad stopped in his tracks. He drew closer and peered at the poster with a curious eye. "Good heavens." He frowned. "What a frightfully unattractive character. Just look at him. A member of the criminal classes if ever I saw one, with those bulbous eyes, those pendulous jowls, that low forehead. And no neck to speak of. I'd better keep a sharp watch out. I'd hate to cross paths with such a shocking villain as that."

He edged around the village green and was just creeping past the stone church when the double doors suddenly burst open and the air was filled with splendid organ music. Majestic arpeggios spilled into the road, cascading one over another like a waterfall.[59] Toad just had time to duck behind the hydrangeas before a merry bridal party

---

59. If your parents inflict piano lessons on you, ignore this footnote. If they do not, an arpeggio is the breaking up of a chord so that the notes are played one after another instead of all at once.

emerged to the accompaniment of many cries of good wishes and many handsful of rice tossed into the air. The bride and groom stepped forth, resplendent in their wedding finery, followed by the parents of the happy couple.

There was something about the father of the groom that seemed direly familiar to Toad. Where had he seen that craggy forehead? What was there about those bushy eyebrows that struck terror in his heart? And the beaky nose, like the prow of a ship? Then it came to him. It was the Magistrate who had peered down on him from his bench and sentenced him to twenty years for assorted high crimes and misdemeanors.

Oh, most miserable of toads! Oh, unluckiest of creatures! If they caught him now, they'd fling him back into England's grimmest dungeon and tack on another ten years for his audacious escape. He would languish there for the rest of his dreary days, growing ever paler and wanner, sleeping on a moldy pallet of damp straw, dining on prison fare of stale crusts and brackish water, one endless year piled upon another. He would never again set eyes on his beloved home, or share a picnic with the Rat on the sunny Riverbank, or indulge in a glass of sherry with the Mole before a crackling fire, or be lectured sternly by the Badger about his many alleged character flaws.

Toad yipped in fear and cowered beneath the bushes. Gone was the puffed-up vainglorious toad of a minute before, and in its place was a timorous, cowering beastie, prostrate in the dirt. He covered his eyes, expecting to be seized by the scruff at any moment.

The minutes passed. Oddly enough, the heavy hand of the law fell not upon his collar. Toad cautiously raised his head and looked about. By a stroke of good luck, the newly married couple, trailed by their celebrants, had turned left coming out of the church, instead of right, and had walked off the other way to the wedding breakfast.[60]

He got up and in short order convinced himself that he had, once again, made a narrow escape from the law due to his quick wits and plucky spirit.

"Why," he said, "they'll never get the best of Toad. They've tried and tried, but they haven't got the best of Toad yet."[61]

He darted behind the church and followed a footpath some distance, then spied a likely shortcut through a grand garden, almost as grand as his own at Toad Hall. He ducked past the maze and circled around a fountain and a small ornamental lake where a brace of

---

60. In England, the wedding reception is called the wedding breakfast, even if it's held in the afternoon. Yes, I know that's odd.

61. Toad is referring to himself here in the third person. This is absolutely insufferable and not to be indulged in by anyone. *Ever.*

serene swans floated by. He was tiptoeing through the grounds when he realized, to his horror, that voices were advancing upon him—he had stumbled into the tulips of the wedding breakfast. In terror, he cast about for a hiding place, but there was none; he was midway down a long expanse of lawn, empty save for several statues in the classical mode and an ornamental garden pond that would scarcely conceal a goldfish.

He was doomed.

And then, without warning or justification, a thunderbolt of uncharacteristic inspiration was delivered from the heavens into the thick skull of our subject. That is to say, Toad suddenly had a good idea. Still covered in fine gray dust from his disgraceful tantrum in the road, he spied an empty plinth near the pond.[62] He leapt upon it and struck a pose and willed himself not to blink.

The Magistrate happened to be an art lover. He circulated leisurely around the garden and inspected the various pieces of statuary: a nymph pouring water from a jar, Poseidon rising from the waves, a deer poised to take flight. And, next to the pond, a toad.

The Magistrate examined it closely and said, "What a lifelike toad. Reminds me of that awful feller who stole that motor-car."

---

62. Plinth: the base or pedestal upon which a statue is placed.

"Most lifelike," said the Magistrate's wife, joining him. "We could find out the name of the sculptor and get one for our garden. Would you like that, dear?"

The Magistrate shuddered. "Gad, Lillian, bad enough that I had to look upon that hideous visage in court. No, no, my dear. I'm happy with our garden just the way it is." The Magistrate and his lady wife linked arms and began to stroll away.

Toad, who had been savagely holding his breath, couldn't believe his ears. Hideous? *Hideous?* Why, he was the handsomest toad in all of England, was he not? His own mirror confirmed this on a daily basis. Surely the Magistrate was mistaken. Yes, that had to be it; the daft old fool had confused him with some other toad.

"You silly old trout," he muttered on his platform, "I ought to come down there and whack some sense into you."

"What was that?" said the Magistrate, wheeling around. "I could swear I heard a voice." He peered about suspiciously. "Sounded awfully like a voice I've heard before. Sounded like that awful Toad feller. I did tell you about him, didn't I, Lillian? A hardened ruffian. An incorrigible rogue. Stole a motor-car and drove it recklessly to the public endangerment. One of the slimiest villains it was ever my misfortune to gaze upon in the dock."

Slimy? *Slimy?* First *warty* from the Master, now *slimy* from the

Magistrate? It was just too much. But through supreme effort of will, the statue bit its tongue and remained mute, as statues typically do.

The Magistrate's wife said, "I hope you threw the book at him, my dear."

"Oh, he got what he deserved. A creature foul and low, Lillian. Most foul and low."

The statue remained motionless, again as statues usually do, bolstered by its memory of the ghastliest dungeon in all the land.

The Magistrate narrowed his eyes at the statue and said, "Hmm, that's odd. I could have sworn the facial expression on this one was different a minute ago. It was most unappealing before, but now I'd say it looks . . . deranged. Looks like it's about to bust a valve. Odd, that."

His wife said, "Goodness, darling, I don't know how you stand dealing with such riffraff all day long. It must be terribly hard on you, but never mind. Let's have some more wedding cake, shall we?"

"An excellent idea." They strolled off to the pavilion.

Toad released his long-pent-up breath with a great *whoosh*.

"Oh," he gasped, "what have I ever done to deserve such shabby treatment? Am I not the most blameless of toads, the most reasonable of toads? Can I help it if people just carelessly leave their motorcars lying about? Can I help it that I'm a toad who was bred for Speed?

It's just the way I was made, so why does the world persist in tormenting me? It's most unfair."[63]

He slipped beneath the hedge and considered his situation. If it hadn't been for the news of Humphrey, he would still be ensconced in his comfortable chambers at college, discoursing on life, the universe, and everything, bestowing the gift of his staggering intellect on the world.

With a jolt, he realized he hadn't given a moment's thought to his nephew. He'd been so busy, first admiring his own cleverness and then feeling sorry for himself, that he hadn't spared a single thought for the poor boy's whereabouts or safety. Where was Humphrey now? Was he hungry? lonely? frightened? Who was looking after him, making sure he ate his porridge in the morning and got his afternoon tea? Perhaps he had been snatched by a gang of ruffians, not one of whom would bother to read him a bedtime story.[64] Perhaps he had wandered off and fallen into quicksand. Were there not tornados and tidal waves? Crocodiles and pythons? What about measles? mumps? gumboils? The many possible fates lying in wait for a toad of Humphrey's tender years were too awful to contemplate. Toad

---

63. Remember the footnote on page 156? The one about life being unfair?

64. It appears to have slipped Toad's mind that his nephew is an excellent reader (in fact, far better than Toad) and is perfectly capable of reading a bedtime story to himself.

pulsed with alternating waves of fear for his nephew's well-being and shame over his own self-centeredness.

After feeling contrite for a full three minutes (unprecedented in his case), he said, "Oh, buck up, Toady. You're of no help to him like this. No, you've got to get home and find Ratty and Badger and Mole. They'll know what to do. But first you require some sustenance, or you'll never make it back."

The wedding guests were departing the grounds, and the servants were cleaning up the remains of the party. Leftover food and drink lay practically at hand if Toad could just keep his wits about him. The footman and maid clearing one end of the pavilion were too busy flirting with each other and exchanging cheeky remarks to notice a short, rotund figure lurking beneath one of the tablecloths. Toad waited until they were roaring over some private joke, then, quick as a flash, he grabbed a half-empty bottle of Champagne, a wedge of cake, and a handful of finger sandwiches, and darted back to the safety of the hedge as fast as his feet would carry him.

CHAPTER SEVENTEEN

Shocking Rudeness

In which negotiations go awry,
and our heroes devise a plan of rescue.

The Mole convened in the library with Rat and Badger.

"I say we storm the Wild Wood with sticks and clubs and just *take* him back," boomed Badger.

"But what if Humphrey gets hurt?" said Mole. "And what if all their clans have joined together? They'll be too many for us to handle."

"Then we'll enlist the otters," said Badger. "And I'm sure we could round up a few more Riverbankers if it came to that."

Mole said, "But *why* did they snatch him? I know it's the Chief Weasel's birthday coming up, but maybe this is actually about something else. Perhaps they want Toad to pay a ransom. Perhaps they want *us* to pay a ransom."

"But," Badger pointed out, "there's been no ransom note, and none of us has any money to speak of. At least, not anything like Toad's money."

"It's true, I don't have a lot of money," said the Rat, before adding hesitantly, "although . . . I suppose my rowboat is worth something. I wonder if they'd take that in trade?" His brow creased in anxiety, for his tiny blue-and-white boat was dear to his heart, and even though he would gladly give it up to save Humphrey, parting with it would mean the end of messing about in boats. A wrenching blow indeed.

"Don't worry, Ratty," said Mole, hastening to reassure his friend. "I'm sure they're not after your boat. It's of no use to them in the middle of the Wild Wood."

The Rat sighed a private sigh of relief.

"Where *is* Toad?" grumped Badger. "If he received the telegram, he should have been here days ago."

"Do you think we should form a search party and go out looking for him?" said Mole.

"No," said Badger, "it's better that we don't scatter. And who knows where he is? He could be anywhere. And remember, it's not as if he's the most useful animal to have around in a crisis. On the contrary, we're probably better off without him." The others nodded ruefully and gazed into the fire.

"I think," said Mole eventually, "that we should try and talk with the Wild Wooders, or at least send them a letter and find out what's behind this. Then we could negotiate for Humphrey's release. What do you say?"

"I say we should go in there with sticks and whack 'em and show 'em what's what," said Badger.

"No," said Rat, "Moly's right. Let's send them a letter. We need more intelligence. Then we can make a proper plan."

Mole poked about and produced a fountain pen and some engraved stationery bearing the legend "Toad Hall" in fine script. "Rightio," he said. "I'll start off, but you two'll have to help me. Hmm, let's see, let's see, how to start. Oh, I've got it. 'Dear Chief Weasel.' How's that?"

"Better add 'and Under-Stoat,'" said Ratty. "We don't want to miff him. I hear he runs the show these days."

A good hour later, Mole had finished composing the letter, and they all signed it.

Dear Mr. Chief Weasel and Mr. Under-Stoat,

We know you have Humphrey in your possession. Are you keeping him safe and sound? If you let him go now, we will forgive and forget. Kindly reply by next post.

Very truly yours,

The Mole, The Badger, The Water Rat

(PS—Please ensure that he brushes his teeth. Thank you.)

The reply came the following day, laboriously scrawled in thick pencil:

Nun of yor bleedin bizniss why we took him.
As for forgiv and forget? Not likly. Badgir has
a long memry.

Very turly yours,
Cheef Weasel and Under-Stoat

(PS—Of cors we see he brushs his teef.
Do you take us for savidges?)

Badger seethed at this response. Mole picked up his pen and said, "Right, then. Let's offer them a carrot." He wrote,

Dear Chief Weasel and Under-Stoat,

Your letter received, and found to be not particularly helpful in providing insight into the current regrettable situation. Is it ransom that you want? We shall go to the bank and borrow five pounds. That should be more than enough to buy him back. We expect you to accept this extremely generous offer. It's more than any of you deserve.

Very truly yours,
The Mole, The Badger, The Water Rat

Badger growled, "Why don't we just promise 'em all a holiday in the south of France?" but nevertheless signed his name.

Came the reply:

Nun of you is worth fiv pouns and evrybody knows it. Be sides, it's not mony we want, so there, Mister Smartee.

Very turly yours,
C W and U-S

Badger roared at the gross impertinence of this reply. The Rat seethed, and the Mole huffed, but nevertheless took up his pen again. "All right," he said. "No more carrots. Now it's time for the stick."

Dear Chief Weasel and Under-Stoat,

Look, you bunch of louts, we've all had it with your rotten behavior, and we expect you to stop it immediately. Let Humphrey go right now, or we will make you regret it. We mean it.

Very truly yours,
Mole and Rat

(PS—Badger refuses to sign; you've made him that cross.)

Came the response:

Oooh, we are all shaken in our boots.
Very turly yours,
You know who

This time, the sheer rudeness of the letter caused even the normally placid Mole to dance about in apoplectic fury. "Well, that was certainly an exercise in futility," he cried, "and it's all my fault. I'm the idiot who suggested it. What a foolish animal I am!"

It was Badger's turn to counsel cooler heads. "Now, Mole, calm down. We have in fact learned something of use. We have learned that they don't want a ransom."

"Then," mulled the Rat, "d'you mean to say that all this uproar is just about fixing the balloon? It seems like a ridiculous amount of trouble for a birthday party."

Badger said with a gleam in his eye, "I think I know what we need. I think we need . . . a spy."

"A spy?" exclaimed Mole.

"But who?" said Rat.

"One of us," said Badger, "in disguise."

"Disguised as who? As what?"

"A tradesman of some sort," said Badger. "Someone who comes and goes through the Wild Wood. Someone they're used to seeing about. Possibly a tinker."[65]

"A fruit-and-veg man," the Rat chimed in.

"A washerwoman!" exclaimed Mole.

Badger looked at Mole approvingly. "An excellent idea, Mole, especially if Toad kept his old disguise. Now, if he did keep it, where would it be?"

"I bet I know," said Rat. "There are trunks full of old clothes in the attic. He keeps them for putting on entertainments."

After a full hour of searching, they stumbled on a collection of

---

65. Tinker: an itinerant mender of pots and pans. You don't see too many of them about these days, but they used to be thick on the ground. Today's pots and pans must be better made.

dusty, cobwebbed trunks. There was no sign of Toad's washer-woman disguise, but the trunks contained a rich treasure trove for playing dress-up: top hats, shabby frock coats, frayed satin gowns, buckled shoes and beaded reticules, even a collection of moth-eaten powdered wigs from another century. One chest contained a fine collection of artificial gems, clattering bracelets of indeterminate metal, chains of dubious gold, and long loops of faux pearls. Sneezing and choking, the three of them hauled their loot to the library.

"Goodness," said Mole, "what an interesting—*ra-ноo!*—bunch of stuff. Where d'you suppose Toad got it?"

"Ancestors," said the Rat, whose nose ran alarmingly.

Badger pulled an old dress and flowery fringed shawl from the trunk and held the items up for inspection. "This would do for a gypsy woman. The only question is, who is going to play her?"

They stared at one another. The idea, which had been so appealing in theory, presented itself in a different light now that the moment of decision had arrived.

"It's a bit like belling the cat, isn't it?" said Badger drily.[66]

---

66. Do you remember this story from when you were young? About the mice deciding that the smart way to protect themselves from the cat was for one of them to put a bell on her collar? And how they all agreed it was a brilliant plan, right up to the moment when one of them had to volunteer for the job?

Rat looked at the clothing and said, "Well, Badger, there's not a chance of you fitting into any of this stuff, so I s'pose it's got to be me or Moly."

Mole gulped and the hair on the back of his neck stood on end. He hoped that neither of his friends noticed.

"And, Moly," Rat continued, "since you had such a bad time of it in the Wild Wood before, I think it should be me that goes."

The Mole gulped again, this time in gratitude.

"Besides," said the Rat, "I've always wanted to play a gypsy. Me for the wild, wandering, Bohemian life! Perhaps I'll even tell a fortune or two."

"This is not a game," said Badger, fixing the Rat with a piercing look. "This is a very serious business."

"Ratty, promise me you'll be careful," said the anxious Mole.

" 'Course I will," Ratty said. "Don't worry about me, Moly. You're not talking to *Toad*, you know."

"Too late to do anything tonight," said Badger. "You'll start out at first light. Now, everyone, off to bed. We all need a good night's sleep. Especially you, Ratty."

Alas, on this night of all nights, it was the Rat's turn to lie awake. For, despite his bold speech, he knew that his mission was fraught with danger. He turned this way and tossed that way, and followed the relentless progression of the clock.

CHAPTER EIGHTEEN

The Old Gypsy

*In which we follow Ratty into the Wild Wood, and we learn
that some weasels are not as bright as they should be.*

The Rat finally fell asleep five whole minutes before Badger shook him awake. Yawning and groaning, he allowed himself to be led downstairs by his friends and dressed in faded finery: a trailing skirt of moldering velvet, patched in many places, the flowery fringed shawl, and several cheap clanking bracelets. This getup was crowned by a scarf of multicolored silk knotted low across his brow and dangling earrings of mock gold.

Mole and Badger stood back and surveyed their gaudy creation.

"Your own mother wouldn't recognize you," said Badger. "You'll do."

"Wait," said Mole. He ran to the weapons room and came back with a pistol and compass and wordlessly offered them to the Rat, who slipped them into his pockets before selecting a stout blackthorn staff for a walking stick and also—perish the thought—as a weapon, should the need arise. They set out single-file in the dark, each wrapped in his own thoughts. By the time they got to the edge of the Wild Wood, the morning birds were tuning up.

Badger gave last-minute instructions. "Remember, Ratty, you must be out before dark, or things could go very badly for you." The Mole was grim and silent, his heart so full of worry for his friend that he could not speak.

Ratty said, "Try not to worry too much, Moly. I'll be all right."

They gravely shook paws. Rat turned and walked into the forest. His friends watched in silence, their eyes fixed upon the gaily colored figure as it grew smaller and smaller, until it finally disappeared, devoured by the impenetrable shadows of the Wild Wood.

By the time the Rat reached the depths of the forest, he had thoroughly transformed himself. He hobbled stiffly, as if his joints ached; he was bent over like a crochet hook; he moved slowly and leaned on his staff for support.

Up ahead, a scruffy, half-grown stoat stepped out from behind a tree and shouted, "Halt! Who goes there?"

"Well," muttered the Rat, "that's certainly original."

"What was that?" cried the sentry.

"I said my name is Seraphina Original."

"That's a funny name," said the stoat. "Wot's the password, then?"

"Password? I don't have any password. I am just an old gypsy woman, as you can plainly see. And besides, young man, it's very rude to remark upon someone's name."

The sentry looked abashed and ground his toe into the dirt. "Sorry," he said.

"That's all right," said the gypsy kindly. "What's your name, anyway?"

"Digby, ma'am."

"Will you take me to your camp, Digby? For I have had a vision that there is a wondrous flying machine hidden in the forest. Do you know of it?"

"Know of it? Why, mother"—here the sentry looked immensely proud—"I'll have you know we've *got* it. The Chief Weasel's promised to make it fly again. He said we could all take turns having a go."

"Is that so?" marveled the gypsy. "Will you take me there?"

"I dunno," said the sentry doubtfully. "I'm not s'posed to let anyone by without the password. I could get in big trouble."

"I understand perfectly, Digby," said the gypsy. "You're only doing your job, and I must say you're doing a fine job for such a young lad. Look, I tell you what. Why don't you just whisper the password to me, and then when you ask me again, I can give it back to you?"

Digby pondered this. There seemed to be something a bit off about this suggestion, but he couldn't for the life of him figure out what. He gave up the struggle and whispered in the gypsy's ear, "It's gob-stopper."[67]

"Good boy," whispered the gypsy, and then said loudly, "You can ask me the password now, Digby."

"Rightio." He took a step back, thrust out his chest, and threw up his arm. "Halt!" he cried in proper military fashion. "Who goes there?"

"No, Digby," said the gypsy mildly. "We've already done that bit. Move on to the next bit."

"Oh ri', ri'. Wot's the password, then?"

"Gob-stopper."

---

67. American: jawbreaker.

"Very good, madam. You may pass." He tipped his cap.

The gypsy hobbled on, thinking that if Digby was the best the Chief Weasel could do for a sentry, the job of recovering Humphrey might not be so difficult after all.

But the next sentry, an adult weasel, was a different story. He was lean and hard-bitten and examined the gypsy with a gimlet eye.

"Password!" he barked nastily.

"Gob-stopper," replied the crone.

"Well, drat," said the weasel. "I s'pose I have to let you pass. Although, old woman"—he paused and looked the gypsy up and down—"there's something not quite right about you. I don't know what it is, but I'll be keeping my eye on you. Proceed."

Ratty thanked his lucky stars for Digby and resolved to go easy on the poor featherbrained stoat, come the time of reckoning. He limped on, taking deep breaths and concentrating on keeping his hackles down, for he was now in the dark heart of the Chief Weasel's territory, where no Riverbanker had ever been. He checked his pockets. The cool brass disk of the compass and the heft of the pistol gave him some comfort. "Right, Ratty," he whispered. "Think of Humphrey."

He soon found himself in a clearing filled with a throng of busy stoats and weasels. So alarming were their numbers that a chill ran through him. Many of them swarmed over some kind of platform they were building. Others rushed first this way with lumber, and then that way with nails. There was a good deal of hammering and shouting and confusion. The platform was already four weasels high and looked as if it was meant to go much higher. In the middle of all the bustle lounged the Chief Weasel, enjoying a biscuit and a cup of tea. At his elbow stood the Under-Stoat, barking orders in a bossy manner and sending the workers scurrying to do his bidding. There was no sign of the balloon. There was no sign of Humphrey.

"Good morning, mother," the Chief Weasel hailed him. "Come and stop for a moment. Sit down and rest yourself. You're no doubt a long way from home."

"Indeed," said the Under-Stoat, examining the gypsy through narrowed eyes. "A long way from 'ome. I don't remember seeing you before. Pray tell us what, exactly, you are doing here?"

"Oh, come now," said the Chief Weasel amiably. "I'm sure there's no need to take that tone. Sit and rest, mother. Cuppa tea?"

"Th-thank you," stammered the Rat in a quavery voice. He lowered himself with gratitude onto a nearby log, for his knees had suddenly become untrustworthy. A cup and saucer were thrust into his paw, and he sipped the strong tea, grateful for an excuse to be silent for a minute. His cup clinked against the saucer. The Under-Stoat glared at him and said, "Why are you all a-shiver, old woman? Why do you quake and tremble so?"

The Rat said in a faint voice, "F-forgive me, sir. I have the palsy, and I have walked far. Just let me catch my breath."

"See?" said the Chief Weasel. "Nothing to bother about, just an old gypsy woman. Collect yourself, mother."

"Yes, do that," said the Under-Stoat mulishly. "And then tell us what brings you here."

"Bikkie?" said the Chief Weasel, offering a plate of biscuits.

"You are most kind," said the Rat. He munched on a piece of shortbread and finished his tea, keeping his eyes lowered but all the while taking stock of the activity swirling around him. He delicately wiped the crumbs from his whiskers and said with growing confidence, "I have come to see"—he paused dramatically—"*it.*"

"*It?*" said the Under-Stoat sarcastically. "Wotcher mean, it? There's no *it* to see here."

The Chief said, "Speak plain, mother."

"I have come to see the flying machine," said Rat.

"What?" they exclaimed, jumping up and demanding, "How did you know?" and "Who told you?" The Under-Stoat looked very menacing indeed.

"G-gentlemen," quailed the Rat, "no one told me. I had a d-dream, a vision, if you will, that there is a flying machine here."

"You can do that?" said the Chief Weasel, impressed.

"Aye, sir. I have the gift of second sight. It comes down on my mother's side in the family. I inherited it from my mother, who inherited it from my granny Lavinia, and my great-aunt Sylvia also—"

"Yes, yes, never mind all that," said the Chief Weasel. "Can you tell fortunes, too? And read palms?"

"Of course I can," said the Rat enthusiastically, getting into his part and letting it carry him away. "Just cross my palm with silver, gentlemen, and you too can know the future. It's like I told you, it runs in the family. Now, my great-great-grandmother Eugenie . . ." He gassed on about his fictitious family tree until, at a signal from the Chief Weasel, the Under-Stoat scampered away and returned a minute later with a small leather bag. The Chief rummaged in it and extracted two silver coins, which he held out to the Rat, who had by now progressed to his great-grand-uncle Algernon. He stopped and said, "Uh, what's that for?"

"It's payment for your services," said the Chief. "I want you to tell my fortune."

"Well, I, um, I'm somewhat rusty, you see," said the Rat, backtracking as fast as he could. "It's been a while, and I'm out of practice.

You wouldn't want your fortune told by someone out of practice, would you? Because it, um, might be defective in some way. I mean to say—"

The Chief pressed the coins into the Rat's paw. "Now," he said, "will you read my palm? Or do you use the cards?"

Ratty protested weakly, "I don't have my cards with me."

"I'm sure we've got a deck around here somewhere, don't we, Under-Stoat?"

"Oh, no, no," said the Rat hurriedly. "That won't work. They have to be special cards, you see, not just ordinary old cards."

"Then read my palm," said the Chief Weasel. He sat down beside the Rat and held out his hand expectantly. "Go on. I've always wanted to have my fortune told."

Rat's thoughts buzzed in his head like bees when the hive is being robbed. He told himself sternly, Ratty, for goodness' sake, grab hold of yourself. You, Rat, are a poet. You are a writer. That means you know how to make things up, right? So make something up now. And make it good.

He studied the weasel's palm.

"This," he said, "is your, ah, life line. Yes. See how long it is? That means you're going to live to be a great old age."

The Chief looked deeply gratified.

"And this one here is your, um, heart line. Yes. And a strong one it is, too. It shows that you have a, er, bold nature. You are unafraid of a fight."

The Chief looked deeply pleased with himself.

"You are, hmm, fearless in battle," said the Rat.

The Chief preened unashamedly and called out to his underlings, "My goodness, this old woman certainly knows her stuff!" and with these words, the Rat realized he'd stumbled inadvertently on the secret of fortune telling, which is that a gullible public will swallow any old nonsense, as long as it is flattering. He larded on the compliments until even the Chief had had enough and interrupted him with, "What about my balloon? Can you see my balloon?"

Your balloon! thought Ratty. *That's cheek if ever I heard it.* He closed his eyes and tried to look as if he was concentrating hard on something. He said, "It's . . . it's a bit faint."

"Is it flying? Do you see it flying?" said the Chief.

"I can't tell. It's too far away," said Rat. "But wait!" He squeezed his eyes tighter and furrowed his brow.

"Go on," urged the Chief. "What do you see?"

"I see . . . I see a small animal . . . doing something. He . . . he appears to be working on it. Repairing it, possibly? Can that be true?"

The Chief and Under-Stoat exchanged glances of disbelief.

"There's something odd about the picture, though," said Rat. "The creature appears to be . . . it's coming clearer to me now . . . not a stoat . . . not a weasel . . . but a toad. How strange. You don't happen to have a young toad in your employ, do you?"

The weasels gawked at him.

"W-we do," stammered the Chief. "He's what you might call a sort of guest of ours."

"I would dearly love to see a flying machine, and if you take me to it, I can tell you if it will fly," said the Rat slyly. "The signal will come in stronger. Is it far from here?"

"Not far at all," said the Chief. "It's just the next clearing over. If you feel up to it, I'll take you there, and you can have a look."

"Oh, yes," said the Rat, jumping up. "I feel positively refreshed. Shall we go?" He dropped the silver coins into his skirt pocket.

"Why, mother, you're walking so much better now," said the Chief. "That cup of tea's done you the world of good. I've always said it's positively medicinal stuff."

Ratty caught himself and leaned heavily on his staff. He sneaked a surreptitious glance at his compass.

"What is that?" said the Under-Stoat suspiciously. "What is that thing that you study in your pocket? Is it a compass?"

"No, no," said the Rat hurriedly. "Well, that is to say, I s'pose it technically *is* a compass, but that's not what I use it for—no, no, not at all. It's more like a talisman, a magical token. It helps me, erm, concentrate my powers."

The Under-Stoat did not look completely convinced, but they set off walking. After five minutes, they came to the edge of another clearing. The Rat's heart beat fast. He slipped his paw into his pocket and grasped the pistol for courage.

On the far side of the clearing lay the balloon, still puddled on the ground, but now with many patches on the canopy. The basket had resumed something of its former shape. A score of weasels, looking very short-tempered, were trying to sort out the tangle of lines, cutting and matching and splicing and generally getting in one another's way. And there, there was Humphrey, perched on a low stool, weaving together a bunch of supple willow twigs.

Ratty studied the small figure bent over his work. Despite a forlorn attitude, the little toad appeared to be well-fed, and someone had given him an oversized cardigan to wear against the chill of the forest. For one wild second, the Rat entertained a fantasy of snatching him up, tucking him under his arm like a rugby ball, and running for their lives, but he knew he'd never make it to the edge of the wood. The plan was squelched for certain when he spotted a thin chain snaking across the ground from Humphrey's ankle to a nearby oak. The Rat's blood boiled. The brutes had chained the poor lad to a tree!

"So," said the Chief Weasel, gesturing grandly, "what d'you see now, mother? Do you see the machine in the air?"

Humphrey paused in his work, turned, and looked at the brightly clad gypsy. In disbelief, he gasped, "What are you doing here dressed like that, Ratty?"

CHAPTER NINETEEN

The Rat in Flight

The Water Rat, mid-flight, has an altogether unexpected encounter.

What does one do when one is in a tight spot? And not just a tight spot, say, but a *really* tight spot? A *really* tight spot that involves, for example, scores of stoats and weasels whose heads all swivel in unison toward one, and whose expressions evolve rapidly from shock to fury? What does one do?

Bluff? Freeze? Run? Hide?

All these questions whizzed through the Rat's brain as he took stock of his situation and measured his chances. He had his blackthorn staff and his pistol, but what good were they against so many foes?

The Chief Weasel goggled in shock.

The Under-Stoat shouted, "I knew it! I knew I smelled a rat!"

Ratty cast a quick glance at the mortified Humphrey, who rocked back and forth, his paws clamped over his mouth in anguish. "Chin up, Humphrey," he called. "We'll be back for you." Then he took off like a shot.

"Not likely!" yelled the Chief Weasel. "Come on, boys—let's get 'im!"

The pack of weasels and stoats tumbled over one another in their eagerness to get 'im, stepping on one another's tails and toes and generally getting in one another's way.

"Don't push! Chief, he pushed me!"

"I did not."

"Yes, you did."

"It wasn't me."

"Yes, it was."

And so forth, the way that an overly excited crowd of stoats and weasels will do, all of which only served to give the Rat a good head start. He took advantage of it and ran as he had never run before. Behind him, he heard the tolling of an alarm bell, no doubt a call for reinforcements.

Soon he came upon the beady-eyed sentry, who cried out, "Halt, who goes there?"

"What bosh!" cried the Rat as he bowled the sentry over and ran on.

Next he came to Digby, who gave him a cheery smile and wave and said, "Good-bye, Seraphina Original. P'raps you can stay for supper next time."

"Good-bye, Digby!" the Rat called over his shoulder (for even when one is on the run, it never hurts to return a courtesy).

The Rat ran until he thought his heart would leap from his chest. He came to a fork in the trail and paused to take a quick look at his compass. He pitched his blackthorn staff down the left fork as far as he could and then hurried away down the right. At the next fork in the path, he threw his shawl down the right and ran to the left.

Some distance back, the weasels and stoats had finally sorted themselves out and were hot in pursuit. The ruses with the staff and shawl bought the Rat a few extra minutes, but soon he could hear a faint whistling behind him, shrill and high-pitched, and he knew they had picked up his track. He slowed to a trot in order to catch his breath and ponder his next move. Behind him, he heard the pitter-patter of many small feet, and the sound caused him to break into a run again. The pattering grew louder and louder, and there was a sudden shout of "We've got 'im now, boys!" The Rat turned and faced the Under-Stoat and his advance party of half a dozen soldiers.

"Surrender!" cried the Under-Stoat. The soldiers elbowed one another and jeered at the Rat and laughed horrid thin little laughs. "Come quiet, now, and we might go easy on you."

"Never," cried the Rat. He pulled the pistol from his pocket and fired a shot just over their heads. His pursuers yowled and flattened themselves to the ground. To Ratty's great satisfaction, the cowering Under-Stoat squealed, "Don't shoot, don't shoot."

"There's more where that came from," Ratty said and backed away, keeping his pistol trained upon them. He took a quick peek at his compass and turned and ran. The pistol had bought him some more time, but how much? How long before the hundred other weasels caught up to the Under-Stoat? How long before the Under-Stoat realized that one rat with one pistol could not possibly keep their great numbers at bay for long?

The overhead canopy of branches was thinning, thus admitting more light, and the undergrowth was becoming easier to negotiate. By his reckoning, he was halfway back to the edge of the wood. He thought of poor Humphrey, a veritable slave, down to his chain, a testament to the Chief Weasel's overweening selfishness. But, the Rat told himself, he had at least found the boy and had seen that he was in good trim, if downcast. (If he had only known how downcast, for at that very moment, Humphrey was weeping the bitterest of tears. Sammy's mother, who was one of the seamstresses working on the canopy, tried to console him with a piece of chocolate cake filched from the Chief's private store, but so wretched was the boy that he left it completely untouched.)

The Rat dashed around a large elm tree and ran smack into a figure on the trail, knocking them both flat to the ground. Loaves of bread flew in all directions. The Rat leapt to his feet, as did the stranger, both prepared for the worst. They gaped at each other in shock. The Rat had run into Matilda. It took him a moment to find his voice, for his brain had quite deserted him. He said, "So terribly sorry!"

She stared at the gypsy and murmured, "Oh, it's you. I know it's you. I'd know you anywhere. But why are you dressed like that? And why did you run away from my burrow that day? And why," she added sadly, "did you never come back?"

These words were as a balm to the Rat's sore heart, but there was no time to revel in the moment. "I can't explain just now," he panted. "The stoats and weasels are after me. And I didn't come back because of your suitor."

Bewildered, Matilda said, "Suitor? I have no suitor—only my cousin Gunnar, who was visiting for the day. I waited and waited for you to come back, but you never did."

The blood pulsed in the Rat's brain, and once again he heard the ancient invisible singers, the vast immeasurable chorus of ancestors chanting, "*You must . . . you will.*"

In the distance, he could hear the baying of his pursuers.

"I must fly," he said. "But I promise you this: I will be back." He took her paw in his. They gazed deeply into each other's eyes and then gently, ever so gently, touched noses.[68]

Then the Rat did the hardest thing he'd ever done in his life. He wrenched himself away and soared off, calling over his shoulder, "I promise you!"

By the time the stoats and weasels had come upon Matilda, they found her resting on a fallen log, her basket of loaves tidily packed at her feet.

"Did you see him?" demanded the Under-Stoat.

"See whom?" she stalled politely.

"The Water Rat. He must have come this way."

"I saw no rat at all." She paused and pretended to think. "Hmm, I did see an old gypsy woman. Surely you don't mean her?"

"That's him! That her's not a her—he's a him, and he's a right evil ruffian. Which way did he go?"

"My goodness, what could you possibly want with that old woman?"

---

68. Reader, perhaps we should look away and allow them a moment of privacy.

"Never you mind. Now, tell me quick, which way did he go?"

Matilda, having watched the Rat head southwest, pointed northeast, and the pack took off, much too busy howling and tripping over themselves to notice that she held her paw behind her back, fingers crossed against such a lie.

⟶ ⟵

It was now fully dark. At the edge of the Wild Wood, the Badger and Mole huddled dolefully beside a signal fire they'd built in hopes of guiding their friend home. Mole gnawed his knuckles and tried not to imagine the worst, but the sun had long set and there was no sign of the Rat. Every now and then, some small nocturnal animal stirred in the forest, causing Mole to lift his head expectantly, only to have his hopes dashed each time. Badger had given up on this hours earlier and merely stared morosely into the fire.

Finally, the poor Mole, whose heart was cracking in two, leapt to his feet and burst out, "They've found him out, I know they have!" He paced back and forth. "We are such fools, Badger. We should never have let him go it alone. The three of us should have marched in, one for all and all for one, and taken our chances. But did we do that? Oh, no. We sent in a poor, defenseless water rat who—"

"Hush," hissed Badger, raising a paw.

"Probably didn't have any idea what he—"

"Hush!" snarled Badger, and so fierce was his command that the Mole shut up immediately. The Badger slowly rose to his feet.

"What is it?" whispered the Mole.

"Do shut up and listen."

The Mole strained to listen with every fiber of his being. And then he heard it. Or rather, *felt* it, for a mole's vibratory sense is exquisitely keen. What he felt was the faintest rhythmical pounding on the ground some distance away in the Wild Wood, a regular pounding as would be made, for example, by a running animal. The Mole threw himself to the ground and pressed his whiskered cheek to the earth, the better to detect the source.

"Can you feel it?" whispered Badger.

"It's getting stronger," uttered Mole softly. "Yes. It's . . . it's . . . coming this way." The Mole leapt to his feet. "Suppose it's him? Suppose it's Ratty? Oh, it's got to be him."

The Badger raised his muzzle and scanned the air.

And now the two animals could hear it distinctly, the noise of a distant animal crashing through the bracken. Was it coming their way? Mole shivered and his teeth clicked. Yes! It was getting closer. And now they could tell that it—the runner—was headed straight for the signal fire, which gleamed like a beacon of hope and safety in the vast blackness of the night.

From out of the forest sprang the Water Rat, fur on end. He fell with a cry on the shoulders of his friends.

"It's you, oh, Ratty, it's you!" cried Mole. "We've been so worried, oh, I can't begin to tell you." Laughing and crying, he embraced the Rat.

The Rat gasped for breath. "My friends."

"Ratty," said Badger somberly, "you gave us both a turn. No, don't try to speak. Let us get you back to the Hall. You can give us a full report once you've got a good meal inside you. Mole, leave off squashing the life out of him."

They half carried the exhausted Rat back to the Hall, changed him into a dressing gown, parked him in front of the library fire with his feet propped up, and fed him a restorative supper of hot thick soup and a glass of sherry.

Mole studied his friend as he spooned up his soup and gradually revived. The Rat was worn and filthy but strangely ebullient. Mole said, "Ratty, I have to say, this has been the longest day of my life, having to sit and do nothing but wait for you all day."

Rat exclaimed, "Has it only been a day? Goodness, it feels like a lifetime. There's so much to tell you. First off, and most important, Humphrey is safe. I don't think they'll harm him, because he's the only one who can fix that wretched balloon."

Rat described the scene in the forest with Humphrey laboring away. When he came to the part about the chain, Badger growled, a hair-raising noise indeed. "I'll tan that Chief Weasel's hide, I will."

"Actually," said Ratty, "I think it's as much the fault of the Under-Stoat as anyone."

"Him too. I'll see both their hides tacked up on the shed."

"Go on, Ratty," urged Mole. "Did they see through your disguise? Start from the beginning and tell us everything."

So the Rat started from the beginning and told them everything. (Well, almost everything.) He told them about limping past the sentries, about reading the Chief Weasel's fortune, which had Mole laughing until he cried, about Humphrey's unfortunate remark that had almost cost the Rat his life. He told them about his terrifying flight and the wily tricks he'd employed to throw his pursuers off course, which greatly impressed the Badger. But when he got to his collision with Matilda, for some reason he could not explain, he glossed over her name, saying only that he had run smack into a baker. There was some part of him that was reluctant to share their moment, that felt it was not for public consumption. Not that Mole and Badger were the public, by any means—no, no, it wasn't that at all. It's just that what had transpired between him and Matilda was something secret. And sacred.

Mole, acutely attuned to his friend's mood, noted that Ratty momentarily faltered at this particular part of the story before picking up the thread of his narration and moving on, ending with his final flight toward the bright dot of the signal fire.

"Let me tell you," Ratty said, "never in my life have I been so glad to see a fire. I can't tell you how it heartened me to know that the two of you were keeping watch. It was sheer genius of you to light it. My dear friends!"

The Rat sniffled, Badger cleared his throat, and Mole brushed away a tear.

"What do we do now?" asked Mole. "If we don't hurry, by the time we get back they'll have moved camp."

Badger said, "We'll send for the otters first thing in the morning. There's nothing left to be done tonight except to let Ratty get a good night's rest."

The Mole yawned and said, "I don't know why I'm so exhausted. All I did was sit and wait."

"And worry," said Ratty. "The worrying can wear a body out, too. Rightio, I'm off to bed. I'll see you in the morning." He took his candle and headed up the stairs.

Badger's head gradually drooped on his chest, and he began to snore quietly. Mole stared unseeing at the fire and somberly wondered what it was that his oldest, dearest friend was keeping from him.

CHAPTER TWENTY

Toad's Transportation

In which Toad finds a way home,
and comes dangerously close to learning a lesson or two.

Toad could feel the pull of the distant River in his blood, in his bones, in his very marrow, but there were so many dangerous obstacles in his path (villages, constables, dogs) that he was forced to make many a tedious zigzag in his course, staying off the main roads as much as possible and using the winding footpaths frequented by the small hedgerow folk.

He was contemplating these many delays and his gnawing hunger (for he had long since finished his stolen wedding provisions) when he rounded a curve in the path and narrowly missed bumping into a small, bedraggled weasel. The weasel carried a stick over his shoulder with a spotted kerchief tied to it. He gaped at Toad in wonderment and said, "Why, it's Mr. Toad. Never thought I'd run into you out here, sir."

Toad was tempted to correct him and remind him that he was, more properly, *Professor* Toad, and should be addressed as such. But on further consideration, he realized that, in light of his recent escapades, he might technically *not* be a professor, and besides, it was too much trouble to figure out whether he was or was not and too convoluted to explain it to himself, let alone someone else. He said, "I've seen you before, haven't I?"

"Yes, sir. I'm Sammy, sir."

Toad said excitedly, "Why, you're from the Wild Wood. Tell me quick, boy, how far am I from Toad Hall?"

"About two days' walk, sir, if you know the shortcuts."

Toad groaned. Two more days of sore feet, an empty tummy, sleeping rough, and running from dogs. The vagabond life was not what it was cracked up to be. He said to Sammy, "You know the shortcuts, do you? Can you lead me home?"

Sammy looked downcast and said, "I . . . I've run away, sir. I can't go back again. I'm going to find my fortune in London."

"Nonsense," said Toad. "Surely your mother's worried sick about you. What could you have possibly done that you can't go back to your family?"

But Sammy only shuffled his feet and would not meet Toad's eye, for he could not bring himself to reveal his part in Humphrey's abduction.

"Well, look," said Toad. "Never mind about going back to the Wild Wood. Just lead me back to Toad Hall. I'll pay you handsomely, and then you can strike out again with some money in your pocket. What d'you say?"

Sammy thought about this. Perhaps it would be one way for him to make up for leading Humphrey into the Wild Wood.

"And we could keep each other company," added Toad plaintively. "It's dashed lonely on the road by oneself."

"Awright, Mr. Toad, sir. I'll show you the way."

"There's a good lad. I say, you don't by any chance have anything to eat on you, do you? I'm absolutely famished."

"I've got a cheese sammitch in me bundle. You're welcome to it, sir."

"Oh, capital!"

They settled in the shade of the hedge, and Sammy presented Toad with his sandwich, a bit battered and squashed. Toad's eyes grew big as saucers as he took the sandwich tenderly in both his paws; a small sob of gratitude escaped him. He took a bite and closed his eyes and chewed slowly and luxuriantly, determined to savor every morsel of this repast, the most sumptuous of feasts, more magnificent than any six-course meal at the Hall. For what could compare with the honest pleasure of a slab of sharp cheese between two simple slices of coarse brown bread, when one has been starved and pursued and hounded for mile upon mile, when one has been a toad *in extremis* for days on end?[69]

"Ah," sighed Toad when he had finished the last crumb. "Thank you, my boy. That was the best sandwich I've eaten in my whole life. Your generosity in my time of need will not be forgotten. Now, shall we be on our way? Lead on!"

The pair trudged off across a meadow. After a couple of miles, Toad said, "We could get home so much faster if I could only, er, borrow a motor-car from someone."

"Oh, sir! You knows how to drive?"

At these words, Toad's old mania for motor-cars, dormant in his brain for so long, stirred.

"Do I know how to drive?" Toad drew himself back and huffed, "Why, my boy, I am a *champion* driver. When I was behind the wheel, they used to call me the Terror of the Highway."

---

69. We could even forgive him for licking his fingers, although in truth this is a terrible habit and should never be indulged in among polite company. On your own is a different story.

Sammy thought about this and wondered if it was all that much of a compliment. "I've never been in a motor-car," he said wistfully.

Toad stopped in his tracks. "Never been in a motor-car? My, my, what an awfully deprived childhood you've had. We must remedy that situation right away."

The mania uncoiled itself and reared its ugly head.

"I tell you what," he said. "If we could only locate a motor-car, you too could experience the glory of it: the hum of the engine before you, the whir of the tires below you, the plume of the dust behind you. The sheer intoxicating thrill as your machine devours the miles and whips across the countryside! Oh, bliss! Oh, joy!" Toad stared into the distance, mesmerized by the silvery vision of winged Speed that his mania, once again flourishing, had constructed for him.

After a full minute, Sammy ventured to say, "Mr. Toad? Are you all right?"

Toad's only response was to murmur faintly, "Poop-poop."[70]

"Mr. Toad, sir?" Sammy plucked at Toad's sleeve.

"What? What was that?" said Toad, coming around.

"Who's going to borrer us a motor-car? And where will we find one out here?"

---

70. Right, all you children out there, stop laughing immediately. Toad is simply mimicking the sound of an old-fashioned car horn. He does this whenever he falls under the intoxicating spell of Speed.

Both of these were valid and difficult questions, the first more so than the second. For Toad's idea of "borrering" differed markedly from the generally accepted definition of the same. Toad sidestepped that thorny question by pretending he hadn't heard it. He responded to the second one by saying, "We'll just have to go back to the main road. I'm sure we could find a suitable conveyance parked at some hotel or tearoom."

"We'll have to backtrack," said Sammy doubtfully. "The main road's over that way." He pointed to the field they had just marched across.

"Well, then, let's be off. Time's a-wasting."

Sammy didn't think so very much of this plan, but he had promised to guide Mr. Toad home, and he would see it through.

They came at last to an inn, the Dabbling Duck, and crept around the back. Parked in the cobblestone yard was a broken-down vegetable truck with patched tires and sagging sides, bearing a full load of cabbages. Toad's eye ignored this unsightly specimen of transportation and immediately lit upon the motor-car parked next to it, a sleek black model of raked silhouette, with deeply tufted red leather upholstery and gleaming brass appointments, all of which served to intoxicate his weak brain. He had never before seen such a fine example of Speed incarnate. In awe he whispered, "Poop-poop."

Sammy, who was just catching on that Toad meant to *steal* the motor-car, hung back and said fearfully, "Mr. Toad? D'you think we should? We could get into an awful lot of trouble."

Toad murmured, "Have you ever seen anything so magnificent in all your life?"

At that moment, the door of the pub swung open and a merry, chattering party of husbands and wives emerged, ready to resume their trip on the open road.

Toad and Sammy ducked behind a barrel in the corner of the yard. And such was Toad's mania that for one deluded second he convinced himself that the couples were headed for the cabbage truck and not the stylish motor-car, for surely the car was Toad's by right of sheer covetousness. Was it not?[71] His spirits plummeted as he watched the husbands hand their wives into the dashing motor-car and drive off in high spirits.

"What a sight," he moaned. "I've not seen that particular model before, but I'll have to order three or four as soon as we get home. I wonder what colors it comes in?"

---

71. Alas, being deluded does not make it so.

Beside him, Sammy breathed a sigh of relief at his narrow miss of aiding and abetting felony theft. (Windfall apples were one thing; motorcars, another.) "It's all right, Mr. Toad, we can walk. I'm used to walking."

Toad made no answer. His beady eyes were trained on the ragged truck; his brain was busy calculating whether the cost to his feet of two days' walk was or was not outweighed by the ignominy of arriving home in a cabbage truck. He could just imagine what the squirrels and rabbits would have to say about that. He might never live it down. But before he could make up his mind, an elderly farmer emerged from the pub and claimed the truck as his own.

"Drat," said Toad. "We should have made a run at that truck while we had the chance. Now I s'pose we'll just have to walk."

They headed out of the yard and passed a shed, in the depths of which they saw a decrepit bicycle propped against the wall.

"Perhaps," said Toad, "perhaps . . ."

They ducked into the shed and looked at the machine. It was of a type no longer made, a velocipede, heavy and primitive with chipped black paint and a rusty chain. Amazingly enough, the tires looked sound and were, on closer inspection, full of air.

A moment later, they were on their way, Toad's feet barely reaching the pedals, Sammy perched in the basket, the wind ruffling his fur.

Over the next four hours, Toad worked harder than he'd ever worked in his soft, pampered life. Sammy couldn't reach the pedals at all, so the burden of their transport fell entirely on Toad's shoulders or, rather, his legs. He pedaled and pedaled until they at last came to Toadsworth, beyond which lay the River.

Toad puffed and pedaled his way along the cobblestone streets, which juddered Sammy up and down fearfully, almost causing him to pitch off. A passing squirrel hailed them with, "So you're back, Toady. But, my word, haven't you come down in the world! From motor-cars and airships to this."

"None of your cheek," puffed Toad. "There's no finer form of transportation than a good old-fashioned bicycle. Good for the lungs, good for the figger. Keeps one svelte."

"Is that right?" retorted the squirrel. "So hard to tell in your case. And a weasel for a figurehead, too. Is that a new fad at Cambridge?"

"Don't you mind him," Toad panted to Sammy, gamely plugging on. "Everyone knows squirrels are common. No"—*puff*—"manners"—*puff*—"to speak of."

Sammy, holding on for dear life, could only answer, "Right-ite-ite, sir-ir-ir."

The exhausted Toad smelled the River. With renewed energy, he made the final push and caught sight of his magnificent ancestral lands and imposing stately home. The many days of fear and exhaustion and hunger came to a head, and it was all he could do not to burst into tears. The front door opened, and the butler ran out, shouting irritably and waving them off. "You, there! The tradesmen's entrance is around the back."

Toad halted the bicycle, and Sammy hopped off. The butler stared in amazement and said, "Oh, sir, it's you! Welcome home. Please forgive me for not—"

Despite his fatigue, Toad gestured magnanimously and said, "Dinner for two, immediately. And hot baths all around, I think. And prepare a room for my guest Sammy."

"Yes, sir," responded the butler. "Right away, sir. Mr. Mole and Mr. Badger and Mr. Rat are in the library. Shall I advise them of your return?"

But there was no answer, for Toad, on hearing these words, had rushed to the library door and thrown it open, reuniting with his friends to shouts of wonder and relief all around.

After Toad had eaten and bathed and rested from his strenuous exertions, and made sure that his young guide had been well looked after and tucked into bed by the housekeeper, Toad sat up with his friends. He listened anxiously to Ratty's description of Humphrey's plight.

He said, "You're sure that he's unharmed? His mother will make mincemeat out of me. It's considered poor form to allow a nephew to be kidnapped when he's left in your care." He paused and thought about this. "But, then," he said, "how on earth was I to know he'd be grabbed by the stoats and weasels? No one could have seen that coming. So I'm hardly to blame, after all." He lit a cigar and proceeded to regale his friends with the long and winding tale of some of his recent adventures: about outsmarting the Magistrate, one of the great legal minds of the land; about snaffling sandwiches and wedding cake; about appropriating a bicycle and soldiering on in the face of stupendous adversity; about—

Badger raised a paw. "Hold up just a minute. D'you mean to say you stole a bicycle?"

Toad squirmed. "I didn't, well, *steal* it per se.[72] It was just . . . carelessly left lying about . . . by someone. I just happened to—"

"By *someone*, you mean the rightful owner?" queried Badger severely.

---

72. Per se: Latin for "in itself."

"Toady," said the shocked Mole, "you didn't steal a bicycle. Did you?"

"Oh, all right," burst out Toad. "But I *had* to. You don't understand the dire straits I was in. No food, no money, no motor-car to carry me home. I tell you, Fate has never dealt me a wickeder hand. I've had *such* a hard time of it." A small tear of self-pity trickled down his cheek.

Mole, who couldn't bear to see any of his friends in distress, patted Toad's paw and said, "There, there, Toady. Perhaps we're being too hard on you."

"Nonsense," boomed Badger. "Toad, you shall find the rightful owner and return the bicycle immediately. And you shall pay him a shilling for its use."

Toad shot up in outrage. "I say! How terribly unfair!"

"Consider it a rental fee," said Badger. "And consider yourself lucky that the Law isn't after you for bicycle theft."

Toad paled. "I hadn't thought of that. You're absolutely right, as usual, Badger. I'll see to it immediately. Anonymously, of course." He peered at Badger timidly. "If that's all right?"

"That'll do, Toad," said Badger. "That'll do. We're glad you're home, but that's quite enough about you. It's time to decide what to do about Humphrey. Ratty, you're being awfully quiet. What do you have to say about all this?"

The Rat, who had only been half listening, said, "Badger, I defer to your judgment in this matter."

Mole looked at him curiously and said, "Ratty, you haven't seemed quite yourself since your day in the Wild Wood."

The Rat avoided his gaze and said, "Hmm. I s'pose not."

"Never mind," said Mole. "No doubt it's the stress of your perilous adventure." He paused expectantly and studied his friend, giving him a chance to speak. "Isn't it?"

"Er," mumbled the Rat, "that's right. I say, I'm feeling a bit peckish.[73] Anyone else for a bite of something?"

---

73. A little hungry. Not ravenously hungry, mind you, but more in need of, say, a light snack.

CHAPTER TWENTY-ONE

Humphrey's Travails

In which Humphrey bears up under hardship and receives
an unexpected message and succor, along with raisin toast.

Humphrey sniffled and wiped his nose on his sleeve.[74] It was just before sunrise, and soon they'd be coming to roust him from his hollow in the base of a tree. Then they'd feed him his breakfast of stacks of hot buttered raisin toast, as much as he could eat. (He couldn't complain about this; it was the one pleasant thing about his captivity.) Following this would be another long day of patching and splicing under the constant supervision of the Under-Stoat's hand-picked guards, who wouldn't let him out of their sight for a second.

---

74. This is awfully bad manners, but I think we can forgive the poor, wee toad under such harrowing circumstances, don't you?

Humphrey pulled his rough woolen blanket over his head. He thought about his mother in Italy and wondered if they'd somehow got word to her about his imprisonment. He rather hoped they hadn't, for there was nothing she could do about it except fret herself to the bone. He thought about Toad and wished more than anything that he could join his uncle at Cambridge, working as his lab assistant and helping to solve the mysteries of the universe. He thought about the gentle Mole and the stalwart Badger, and he thought about the daring, audacious Rat, which prompted him to burst into tears, for he—Humphrey—had given the game away and placed the Rat in terrible danger through his own careless words. For this he would never forgive himself. Had Ratty made it to safety? He must have, for the Chief Weasel and Under-Stoat had returned to camp in an unspeakably foul mood, with no Rat yoked between them. But still.

"Hoy, you," said a harsh voice. "Time to get up."

Beneath his blanket, Humphrey wiped his eyes. It was important to him that they not see him cry.

Plucky little fellow!

"Have a wash and don't forget to brush your teef. But hurry up. We're on the march."

Humphrey obeyed and wondered, not for the first time, why his captors always seemed to be nagging him about brushing his teeth.

He emerged from his tree into the clearing where a hectic swirl of preparations was taking place.

"No time for breakfast," said the Under-Stoat. "We're moving. Such a bovver.[75] That gypsy—I mean the Water Rat—had a compass. I tried to tell the Chief that she—I mean he—didn't seem just right, but would he listen to his second-in-command? No. He would not." The Under-Stoat snorted, but not loud enough for the Chief to hear. "So now we've got to pick up and move. Such a bovver. And I've got to get forwarding addresses to the baker and the newspaper boy and the fruit-and-veg man. Oh, look out. Here comes the baker. Get back in your hole."

Humphrey disappeared into his hole just as Matilda emerged on the other side of the clearing.

"Good morning, Under-Stoat," she greeted him. "I have your order here and your bill." She looked about her and said, "Heavens, everyone's in such a tizzy. Are you moving camp?"

The Under-Stoat studied her and said churlishly, "Wot d'you need to know for?"

The baker replied sweetly, "Where am I to deliver the bread? And don't forget the Chief Weasel's birthday cake. He's ordered the biggest cake on record."

---

75. Such a bother.

"Oh. Ri'," replied the Under-Stoat. "Yeah. We're moving to our winter quarters."

"It seems awfully early for that," she said. "Why, there's only the first hint of autumn in the air."

"It's just temporary, mind."

"Very well," she replied, and then presented a bill for the Under-Stoat to sign with his mark, a big, wavering X. Once she had left the clearing, Humphrey was ordered out of his hole again and made to supervise the packing of the balloon in the gardener's second-best wheelbarrow.

Before they set off, he was blindfolded. Digby, who had been placed in charge of him, led him by the sleeve and quizzed him the whole way about Toad Hall, prattling on about its many fascinating modern conveniences and appurtenances. Hot water straight from the tap? Never! A patch of lawn just for croquet? Garn![76]

A half hour later, they arrived at their destination, and Humphrey's blindfold was removed. He blinked in the light. He was standing before a stout, wooden door with no welcome mat or bell, set inconspicuously in the roots of a giant elm and partly concealed by a tangle of bracken. The door opened with a sharp creak, and the Chief Weasel led the way as the others followed single-file.

---

76. Go on! (Meaning, you're joking.)

Humphrey, whose eyes, unlike his captors', were not especially suited to the dark, stumbled along a dark passage with the press of earthen walls on either side. Down and down they went until finally they came to a halt where the faintest of cool breezes blew across his skin. He pulled his cardigan tighter.

They entered a vast hall carved out of the earth, dimly lit by a distant shaft of sunlight. Humphrey gasped at the size of it, the vaulted ceiling so high above him that its farthest corners remained shrouded in shadow. Enormous stone pillars and arches supported the great space; the floor was made of large blocks of quarried stone, tilted and broken in places by thick, gnarled knuckles of ancient roots.

"Digby," he said in wonder, "what is this place?"

"Wot, this?" Digby looked around as if he'd never noticed it before. "It's just where we spend the winter. The elders say it used to be a city of men, invaders from across the sea, hundreds and hundreds of seasons ago, but I wouldn't know anyfing about it. You say that *everyone* at Toad Hall gets his own featherbed? All to himself?"

The weasels set rushlights in brackets the length of the hall; wavering flames revealed patchy expanses of scabby plaster covered with painted figures, now much faded. Humphrey drew closer and saw that the figures were those of dark-haired men and women wearing, for some odd reason, bedsheets. The men wore short armor and carried swords. There were harvest scenes and scenes of celebration.

There were horses and sheep and cattle, and a hunched black-and-white shape much disfigured by time that could have been a sheepdog (or possibly a badger, if one squinted and tilted one's head to the side). He stepped closer to a spot where the paint seemed brighter and tentatively rubbed it with his sleeve. The dust of eons fell away, and he realized he was looking not at painted plaster, but at a mosaic composed of hundreds of tiny tiles, their colors still vibrant, all painstakingly butted together to form the portrait of a man. The man wore a white sheet draped over one shoulder; a coronet of golden leaves sat on his dark curly hair. Humphrey was trying to make sense of this when the Under-Stoat called out, "Hoy! As soon as you can see fit to drag yourself away, young sir, there's a job waitin' for you over 'ere." Humphrey resolved to make further study of the remarkable murals just as soon as he could.

Despite being fatigued, he slept poorly that night, his dreams filled with strange images of an ancient civilization where men wore sheets and crowns of laurel leaves.

∽✦∾

The next morning, there was a general slackening of Humphrey's supervision. The passageway was patrolled by a couple of hard-case weasels, and since there was nowhere else for him to go, he was allowed to work without being chained up, with only the occasional perfunctory glance in his direction. Thus, when the baker made her rounds, no one paid any attention to him and no one demanded he hide himself. He was sitting at the kitchen table and eating his usual breakfast of buttered raisin toast when she arrived with her basket. She started in surprise when she saw him and then deliberately looked away. No one noticed that, either. Humming, she slowly unpacked her ambrosial goods.

The Under-Stoat came in. "Here's the bill for your signature, Under-Stoat," she said sweetly.

"Exorbitant as usual," he said, scrawling his mark. In response, Matilda offered him a cinnamon bun, saying, "I've got a few left over today. Would you like one?"

"Wot's the charge, then?"

"It's *gratis*."

"Wot?" he said suspiciously.

"There's no charge. It's free, to help you keep your strength up. I know how hard you work, how much responsibility you have."

The Under-Stoat snatched the bun from her and crammed it indelicately into his mouth. While he chewed and smacked in loud pleasure, the baker turned to Humphrey and said, "I have another one left over." She reached across the table and placed the bun on his plate.

Despondently, he said, "Thank you," for unlike *some* creatures we could mention, he tried to be an animal of good manners.

Pretending to repack her basket, she bent low and stared into his face with an arresting wide-eyed gaze. He looked at her quizzically. Then, when she saw that she had his full attention, she gave him a slow, intense . . . wink.

Now, there are winks, and there are winks, and this one was not just any old wink, but a wink laden with meaning. A *significant* wink, clearly meant to telegraph information from the winker to the winkee, whose thoughts upon receiving it raced and ricocheted in confusion. Humphrey raised his eyebrows at her in hopes of receiving clarification, but there was only time for her to give him a barely perceptible nod before turning away to gather up her things and bid everyone good day.

Humphrey sat, electrified. He knew he'd been delivered a message, but what did it mean? What—*specifically*—did it mean? He turned the puzzle over and over in his mind, inspecting it from this way and that. After a few minutes, he decided it didn't matter that he couldn't discern its specific contents. The *important* thing was that she'd told him to take heart. She'd told him to have hope. That, in some remote location, plans were being hatched in his favor; forces were plotting his rescue. And all he had to do was watch and wait. Keep his wits about him, and watch and wait.

He studied his plate and allowed himself the smallest of smiles at his bun.

CHAPTER TWENTY-TWO

Plotting and Planning

In which a plot is proposed by an unexpected conspirator,
and possibly derailed by an unexpected spy.

Plans for Humphrey's rescue were indeed being hatched at Toad Hall by our own four friends, but at a somewhat-slower-than-hoped-for pace. They sat in the conservatory and mulled over their next step.[77]

"I'm sure they'll have moved him by now," said Ratty. "How are we going to find him?"

"It's simple," declared Toad. "I will apply my massive intelligence

---

77. A conservatory is a room built of glass, which serves as a greenhouse and is filled with trees and delicate plants. It's also a nice place to sit and take tea.

to suss out his location. Although," he added, "my mind has been working in strange ways lately. My pressing interest in the Great Big Questions seems to have evaporated, which I don't understand at all. But I'm sure that I can muster up more than enough brainpower to calculate the best way of bringing my dear nephew home. Hmmm, let's see." He stared at the ceiling as if the answer might lie there. "Hmmm," he said again. There was no sound but the ticking of the mantel clock; the seconds stretched into several long minutes before Toad came out with his next profound statement, which went like this: "Hmmm."

Rat and Mole and Badger exchanged puzzled glances.

Finally, Toad said, "I'm having trouble concentrating these days. I haven't been myself since I got beaned with that cricket ball."

"Since you what?" said Ratty.

"I got hit on the head with a cricket ball during what turned out to be my last day as the Lumbagian Professor. Frightfully bad luck, what? Now that I think about it, it happened during my last few minutes, mere moments before the Master relieved me of my duties. He behaved frightfully. You'd think a man of his stature would have more compassion for the gravely injured."

"Ah," said Rat, nodding slowly. "Perhaps that explains it."

"Explains what?" said Toad.

By then it was apparent to them that the Poffenbargered Toad had been banished forever—de-Poffenbargered, if you will—and that the dim, familiar Toad of old had slipped back into his rightful place.

"Just when we need the extra brainpower," muttered Badger.

"Explains what?" said Toad.

"Never you mind, Toady," soothed Mole. "You're back among friends where you belong. Now, how will we ever locate Humphrey?"

Came a feminine voice in reply: "I know exactly where he is. And I know how to get him back."

They looked up. The voice belonged to Matilda Rat, who stood silhouetted in the garden doorway with her now-empty basket over her arm.

Our heroes, momentarily nonplussed, stared at her. Toad leapt to his feet and pulled out a chair, prattling on about would she take tea, and did she take milk or sugar or lemon, and would she please sit here in this chair as it had the nicest view of the garden and the comfiest cushion. Badger made a small, courtly bow. The Rat affixed his gaze on his feet as if they had suddenly turned into objects of extreme fascination. Only his closest friend could have seen that his shy demeanor concealed a joyful heart. His closest friend, the Mole, *did* see this, and his own heart inexplicably sank.

Once Matilda had been ensconced in the best chair and supplied with a cup of tea and a plate of biscuits, Badger called the meeting back to order. "You've seen Humphrey?" he said.

"Is he all right?" broke in an anxious Toad.

"I saw him just this morning," she replied. "And he seems perfectly fit. Somewhat despondent, perhaps, but otherwise healthy and well fed."

Toad sighed in relief at the news. "Thank goodness! His mother would knock my block off if he came to any harm."

While Matilda told her tale of her visit to the winter quarters, the Rat studiously avoided looking at her, and the Mole studiously avoided looking at the Rat. Badger studied them keenly in turn. Only Toad seemed oblivious to the electric current that ran between them.

At the end of her report, Toad moaned, "What'll we do? We'll never get him out of there."

"Ah, but we will," said Matilda. "There's something more you need to know. It's the Chief Weasel's birthday in two more days, and he's going to have a huge party. He's determined to take a flight in the balloon to celebrate—that's why they're working Humphrey so hard. And the Chief's ordered the biggest birthday cake known to man. In fact, I should be at the bakery starting on it now, it'll take me that long to finish. I've given this all a good deal of thought," she said, putting down her teacup, "and I've come up with a plan."

At this tantalizing news, everyone edged his chair closer and leaned in. Even the Rat finally lifted his gaze and listened intently.

⤳⤳⤳

Upstairs, the small, bedraggled weasel known as Sammy sat on the bed in the guest room he'd been assigned and looked about him in wonder at the opulent splendor of the furnishings. What would his mam give for a length of the brocade bedspread or a yard or two of the silky fringe hanging from the curtains? She'd probably swoon in delight. Maybe he could snag a bit of it for her. Just a short bit so's no one would notice.

No sooner had this thought popped into Sammy's head than he was overcome with shame. Mr. Toad had been good to him, had given him half a crown and a pat on the head and a soft bed to sleep in and as many slices of lemon cake as he could hold. No, nicking a bit of tassel was no way to repay such a generous host. Sammy stared out the window at the kitchen garden and watched his old nemesis, Cook, gather her vegetables for the next meal. But this was not entertainment enough for a restless young weasel, and he soon cast about for something to do.

By the bedside there was a thick book, which he opened without much hope, for he knew that thick books generally contained large amounts of dense print and few, if any, pictures, and Sammy had not yet reached that point in life where he could appreciate such a volume. He examined the cover: there was a boy, curiously unclothed, surrounded by a bear, a panther, and a wolf. But instead of looking afraid of these fearsome animals, as any sensible boy would, this particular boy lounged against the great bear's furry flank. Sammy shuddered and put the book away. He went to the door and peered along the long hall. There was no one in sight. He slipped next door into Humphrey's room and looked about. There was the tin box of powder, covered all over in warnings. There were the glass beakers and test tubes and flasks. And there was the kite they'd built and launched together, the newspaper now yellowed, the paste now cracked. Sammy backed out of the room, his small, bedraggled heart in turmoil about the part he'd played in Humphrey's imprisonment. He trotted silently down the grand staircase and found the butler, who informed him in very superior tones, "Mr. Toad is in the conservatory with guests." The butler added with a pinched expression (for he was one of those types dead set against weasels in the house), "And I'm sure he does not wish to be disturbed."

"Rightio, guvna," said Sammy.[78] "I'll just have a stroll around the garden." He sauntered outside and, as soon as he was hidden from

---

78. Governor, a slang term of respect.

the butler's frowning gaze, scampered around the wing of the house until he reached the open door of the conservatory, whence issued the inviting sound of tinkling teaspoons and the light clash of crockery. He considered inviting himself in to share whatever bounty the tea tray might yield, but then he heard a deep, resonant voice that could only be that of Mr. Badger, sounding very grim. Sammy flattened himself in the flower bed, for there was no more serious voice in the world than that of Mr. Badger speaking seriously. The words sounded like "winter quarters." And then Mr. Rat said something like "heavily guarded . . ." Then Mr. Mole said something that sounded like "but how can we . . ." And Mr. Toad said "use my brainpower . . ."

A moment later, Sammy heard a voice unknown to him, higher and lighter than the others, but calm and determined. Who could that possibly be? He crept closer. The voice said the words "birthday cake . . ."

Sammy pricked up his ears, for not only is a youngster naturally interested in all matters connected to birthday parties in general (and birthday cake in particular), it suddenly occurred to him that they were discussing the Chief Weasel. He slithered on his belly to the open door.[79]

---

79. You might think that only snakes can slither, but if you've ever seen a member of the Family Mustelidae in action, you'll know what I mean. They are unbelievably bendy and pliable.

Badger said, "It's sheer genius, Miss Matilda. My hat's off to you."

The feminine voice said, "Thank you, Mr. Badger. I'll need an extra pair of hands to help me make it large enough. Who will volunteer?"

The Rat said, "I will," before anyone else had a chance to speak.

There was a significant pause in the conversation. Sammy, whose curiosity was devouring him, raised his head and peered around the thick leaves of a banana tree. And found himself staring directly into the eyes of Mr. Toad, who was staring directly back at him.

"Eep," said Toad in surprise.

"I beg your pardon?" said Mole.

"I say, there's Sammy at the door," said Toad faintly.

They turned in time to see the small head duck below the shrubbery.

"Why, hullo, young Sammy," said the Water Rat. "What are you doing there?"

Caught, Sammy emerged, red with embarrassment. He saw that the female speaker was a lady rat; she looked familiar somehow, but he couldn't think why. Of more pressing concern were the others, who were inspecting him with expressions ranging from concern to animosity. His eyes darted from one to the other, trying to gauge exactly how much trouble he was in. Unfortunately, this only made him look furtive and shifty.

Badger, he of the severest expression, rumbled, "Peeking around corners, that's what he's doing. Spying, that's what he's doing."

"Now, Badger," said Mole. "I'm sure there's some other explanation. Isn't there, Sammy?"

Sammy stuttered, "I was just . . . I was just—"

Badger said, "Peeking and spying." He turned to Toad and muttered quietly, "Go and get him. Who knows what he overheard?"

Toad got up casually and sauntered to the door. "Sammy, come in and sit down."

"Oh, that's all right, Mr. Toad." Sammy backed away across the lawn.

"Be a good boy and come and join us."

"No, no, really, that's all right." Sammy backed away faster.

Toad broke into a trot and called out cheerily, "There's chocolate biscuits."

Sammy turned and also broke into a trot, calling politely over his shoulder, "That's nice."

"You could have some," puffed Toad, slowing to a walk.

"Really, it's all right," said Sammy, also slowing to a walk, but being careful to maintain a healthy distance between them.

Toad broke into a trot again, and so did Sammy.

Toad wheezed, "Why are you running away?"

"I'm not running away. Why are you chasing me?"

"I'm not chasing you. Now, stop running away. Come back and have some lemonade."

"Thanks, Mr. Toad, not really thirsty."

The Rat and Mole and Badger emerged from the conservatory and looked as if they were about to join in the stuttering procession, at which point Sammy wisely weighed his options, which included facing the possible wrath of the Badger. Not liking that particular option *at all*, he took off like a shot for the trees, a blurred streak of grayish-brownish fur.

Who knew a small, bedraggled weasel could run so fast?

CHAPTER TWENTY-THREE

The Trojan Cake

*In which Matilda's ingenious plan unfolds
(and in which there are a few mushy bits, but not too bad).*

The intrepid Matilda temporarily moved her bakery to the kitchens of Toad Hall to avail herself of the cavernous oven built a century before to accommodate a whole roast ox. For the next two days, our heroes busied themselves with secret preparations. The Rat in particular slaved away under Matilda's direction, mixing huge vats of butter and dozens of eggs with a paddle and sifting veritable mountains of flour until he was quite covered with the stuff, leaving him looking like a ghost. He lifted and carried, he sieved and stirred, but instead of being exhausted and miserable, he was exhausted and exhilarated; he pitched into bed at night with a wide smile on his face.

Mole and Badger conferred in a corner of the library, pored over dusty maps of the various trails and tunnels known to lead in and out of the Wild Wood, and debated the merits of alternate routes of attack and escape. They debated whether Sammy had recognized Matilda, and whether or not there was anything they could do about it.

Toad rounded up pistols and stout sticks and ancient swords for each of them. He stumbled on a stray collection of various pieces of pitted, ancestral armor in one of the storerooms and hauled it downstairs to the library, intent on assembling a suit of armor for each of them.

"Look, you chaps," he said, holding up a sixteenth-century shield and seventeenth-century gauntlets. "I think we'll have to mix the centuries to fit us all. It's generally not done, not being historically correct and all, but you fellows won't mind, will you?"

"Toad," said Badger, "I'm not wearing armor, and that's that."

"But, Badger, whyever not?" Toad buckled himself into a heavy iron cuirass to protect the chest, followed by heavy iron greaves to protect the legs, followed by a heavy iron helmet with a visor that squeaked when he lowered it.

All followed by Toad falling facedown on the floor with a resounding crash.

"That's why not," said Badger.

With great effort, Toad managed to roll over on his back, where he lay squirming and thrashing like a large metallic beetle. "Uh," he said, "I say, you two . . . I . . . uh . . . can't get up."

"Exactly," said Badger.

Mole took pity on Toad and helped the clanking creature to his feet. "Perhaps Badger's right," he said. "We probably don't need armor."

"Oh, all right," pouted Toad. Always the mercurial animal, he suddenly brightened and said, "What about horses? And cannon? Can't we have horses and cannon?"

Mole said, "I don't think we need those, either. Especially since we're embarking on a campaign of stealth and secrecy. No, no, they'd hear us coming from miles away. Er, why don't you go down to the kitchen and see if Ratty and Matilda need a hand?"

"I did," said Toad. "They told me to come up here and see if you and Badger need a hand."

"Ah. I see."

The wonderful fragrance of baking cake wafted into the room. Toad sniffed deeply and said, "Smells like they're well under way. I wonder if Miss Matilda will let me lick the spoon?" He wandered back down to the kitchen and found Matilda and Ratty struggling to extract a huge golden cake from the giant oven.

"Good heavens," said Toad. "I had no idea it would be that size."

Matilda mopped her brow with her kerchief and said, "And this is only the first layer. It's going to be three layers tall once I"—she glanced at Ratty—"that is, *we* finish making it. The Chief said he wanted the biggest cake on record, and he's going to get it."

"It's going to be big, all right," said Ratty, beaming at her.

"And full of surprises," added Matilda. "Shocking surprises."

Ratty said, "Three shocking surprises, in fact."

A trifle nervously, Toad asked, "You, er, will be making plenty of air holes, right, Miss Matilda?"

"Of course, Mr. Toad. Don't you worry about that. It wouldn't do to smuggle you in half smothered. You'll need to be in tip-top condition when you arrive."

"I still wish I could talk you out of coming, Matilda," said Ratty, gnawing his lip.

"Nonsense," she said, patting his paw and looking at him fondly. "I know you mean well, Ratty, but I'm the only one who knows the way. And I'm the only one who can get you in. Let's have no more talk about it. Now, I need three more pounds of butter, and there's none left in the larder. Will you run to the shop for me?"

It's a good thing the Mole wasn't there to see it, for the Rat leapt to his task so enthusiastically you'd have thought there was no higher meaning and purpose in life than to run to the shop for three pounds of butter.

⌾

At sunrise the next morning, our team gathered in the kitchen to assemble the enormous cake, almost three weasels high. Matilda cunningly excavated each layer with a long, sharp knife before they stacked the layers one atop the other. She then took a large wooden spatula, practically the size of an oar, and slathered a thick layer of white icing over the entire cake. Finally, she took a thin rod and poked several small air holes in each layer.

"There," she said, "that should be adequate for your needs. And by the time I've finished with the icing, you won't be able to spot the holes." She filled her piping bag with pink icing from a barrel. "Come back in an hour," she said. "And don't forget to bring a stepladder."

The team of warriors returned to the library for a final look at their maps and a final talk of strategy.

"Remember," said Badger, "don't move a muscle until they've finished singing. Then the Chief'll blow out the candle and everyone will cheer. That will be your signal."

"What if we can't hear inside the cake?" said Toad.

"I'll be standing by, and I'll thump on the top," said Badger. "Believe me, you'll hear that."

The butler entered and announced, "Miss Matilda is ready for you."

They picked up their weapons and trooped down to the kitchen to find their singular conveyance covered in pink and blue rosettes. Their machine of war looked like nothing more than an enormous—and innocent—birthday cake. They examined it and praised Matilda's handiwork.

"It's perfect!" exclaimed the Rat. "Why, if I didn't know any better, I'd be completely taken in."

"It's a Trojan horse, er, cake," said Mole.

"Well done," said Badger.

"Erm, there are plenty of air holes, right?" said Toad.

Matilda beamed at their praise. They carefully loaded the cake onto the gardener's first-best wheelbarrow. Toad and Mole climbed up the stepladder and gingerly lowered themselves into the hollowed-out interior, taking pains not to smudge the icing. Then it was the Rat's turn. But first he took Matilda's paws in his and said, "We are embarking upon a dangerous mission. If anything should happen, promise me you'll save yourself."

"I promise," she said. They gazed deeply into each other's eyes and then tenderly touched noses.

Badger looked away and cleared his throat. "Time to go," he said gruffly.

The Rat lowered himself into the cake, but not before bestowing upon his beloved a last look that spoke volumes. Badger hoisted the false top and eased it into place. From inside the cake came muffled complaints: "You're squashing me!" "Move over!" "I *am* over!"

"Settle down, you lot," ordered Badger, and there was immediate silence. Matilda piped a last ribbon of icing around the seam. She circled the cake, examining it with a critical eye, and found everything satisfactory. "Right," she said. "There's only one last thing . . ." She retrieved a large apron and neckerchief and white cap from the scullery and gave them to Badger, who put them on to play the part of her assistant.

"Here we go," said Badger. He hoisted the wheelbarrow's handles.

"Steady on!" came the faint complaint.

"Be quiet," said Badger. "We've got a long trip ahead of us, and I don't want to hear a single word on the way. Not one. Understood?"

Silence reigned.

Matilda took up her basket. It contained two long French baguettes, each of which cleverly concealed a long stick. She opened the kitchen door for Badger and his burden, and they set off, headed for the darkest heart of the Wild Wood.

CHAPTER TWENTY-FOUR

The Big Birthday Party

In which the Chief Weasel, and our heroes,
all receive a nasty surprise.

The voyage of our heroes and heroine was fraught with danger, but not of the kind found in your typical adventure story. For one thing, the fragile icing on the cake had to be protected from the destructive swish of overhanging branches, and Matilda had to plug on in front of Badger to clear the way. For another, the day was warm-ish, which had a deleterious effect on the comfort and morale of the three warriors confined inside the unorthodox vessel, resulting in the occasional faint expostulation, accompanied by a muffled thump, that may or may not have been the sound of one animal elbowing another in the ribs.

"Be quiet. There may be spies about," hissed Badger. "How on earth are we to explain a talking cake?"

Someone—possibly Toad—muttered a retort, possibly something about the heat.

"If you don't shut up immediately," said Badger, "I'm going to plug up your air holes."

Someone—possibly Toad again—mumbled something that might have been "Sorry."

"We're getting close," said Matilda, speaking in a low voice directly into one of the holes. "The tradesmen's entrance is in the next clearing, so get ready. All set, Mr. Badger?"

"All set, Miss Matilda."

"Right. Here we go."

They pushed on into the next clearing, where there was a roughly lettered sign that said TRADSMENS ENTRANS ONLEY.

Matilda took a deep breath, smoothed her apron, and nodded once at Badger, who nodded back. She rang the bell.

From deep within, they could hear the pattering of weasel feet. The door burst open, and there stood the Under-Stoat. He scowled at Matilda and said, "Just in time. We was just about to start, and how would that be without the cake?" He eyed the silent, hulking figure of the assistant baker and said suspiciously, "Who's that, then?"

"Who? This?" said Matilda airily. "Why, it's just my assistant. He helps me at the bakery."

"Never seen him before. Wot's he doing here?"

"Look at the size of this cake. You don't think I could possibly move it here all on my own, do you?" Disdain positively dripped from her.

"Wot's 'is name, then?"

Matilda said, "His name is, um, Igor." She grandly tossed her head and pushed by, saying, "Follow me, Igor." Igor trundled along in her wake.

They soon arrived in the kitchen alcove and found several younger stoats and weasels in the midst of twittering preparations, cutting dozens of sandwiches and mixing a large bowl of punch.[80] They briefly gawped in admiration at the cake and then scurried out into the main hall, bearing their platters of food.

Matilda searched the kitchen for Humphrey, but to her dismay, he was nowhere to be found. "He's not here," she whispered to Badger. "I expected him to be right here. Where could he be?"

Badger looked out into the great hall, where hundreds of stoats and

---

80. I mean twittering in the old-fashioned sense. Stoats and weasels did not possess cell phones until much later.

weasels sat at long tables, feasting and toasting, and clinking their glasses, and stamping their little feet, and pounding the tables with their little fists. At the head table, under a spangled banner reading HAPY BIRFDAY TO THE CHEEF WEASEL! caroused the Chief, the Under-Stoat, and his henchmen. All wore crowns of brightly colored crepe paper, except for the Chief, who wore a crown of gold cardboard.

Badger said, "They're waving at us to come out."

"Just let me light the candle," Matilda said loudly. She struck a match and, just at that moment, a small, bedraggled weasel emerged from a dim side passage.

Sammy and Matilda stared at each other in shock. But instead of running for the head table, Sammy turned on his heel and bolted back the way he'd come, disappearing from sight.

"Ouch!" said Matilda, dropping the spent match. "Oh, dear—he's placed me."

"Then we must act quickly," said Badger, "before he raises the alarm."

"But what's he doing? Where's he going?"

"No time," said Badger. "They're waving us out."

Just at that moment, the crowd in the hall broke into the traditional weasel birthday song.

For he's a jolly good weasel,
For he's a jolly good weasel,
For he's a jolly good weassssseeeeelllllllllll,
Which nobody can deny.[81]

Matilda struck another match and stood on tiptoe to light the candle. Together, she and Badger wheeled the cake into the hall to a great round of applause.

"Cor, what a lovely cake!" "I never seen one that size!" "Enough for me, but what are *you* going to have?" "Har, har!"

Inside the cake, our three cake-onauts heard the roar go up.[82] They grasped their cudgels tighter.

And then . . .

The song went on.

And then . . .

The song went on and on.

Eight minutes later, the candle had burned down and been replaced by Matilda three times over. Her smile grew fixed and began

---

81. Sung, as you may have gathered, to the tune of "For He's a Jolly Good Fellow." However, what differentiates the weasel version is that there are an *interminable* number of verses, so many that even the weasels themselves get tired of it.

82. Yes, I'm aware *cake-onauts* isn't a real word, but under the circumstances, it should be, don't you think?

to resemble a grimace. Inside the cake, Rat's whiskers twitched with nerves, Mole had a nasty cramp in his foot, and Toad was perspiring freely. Matilda's fixed smile grew ever more desperate, and even the Badger, normally the most stolid of animals, looked somewhat wound up.

Finally, *finally*, the Chief Weasel himself got sick of the song and signaled for its conclusion. He descended from the dais and tried to blow out the candle, but the cake was too tall for him, and the Under-Stoat had to fetch a chair. The Chief Weasel climbed up on it. He leaned over the cake, took a deep breath, and blew out the candle. A tremendous cheer went up.

"Now!" bellowed Badger. With a mighty roar, he flung off his cap and apron and grabbed one of the long baguettes. Inside the cake, our trio heard their signal and flung themselves upward against the lid. Which budged not an inch.

CHAPTER TWENTY-FIVE

The Big Birthday Battle

In which a bread stick and quick thinking save the day.
And in which friendship is repaid.

Silence fell in the great hall, unbroken except for distant cheering from the children's table in the far corner, where the celebrants were either too short to see what was going on or too young to understand the calamity unfolding before them.

The Chief Weasel, eyes bulging in disbelief, finally collected his wits and shrieked, "Help!" The Under-Stoat shrieked, "Treachery!" The henchmen shouted, "A spy! A spy!"

Courageous Badger, that stouthearted fellow, found himself standing alone against hundreds, but did he hesitate? He did not. He swung his baguette at the Chief Weasel, who squealed in dismay and beat a hasty retreat around the head table to hide behind the Under-Stoat.

The Under-Stoat studied Badger with cruel eyes and said, " 'Ere all alone, are you, Mr. Badger? Wot a pity your friends ain't here to help you. Get 'im, boys!"

The reluctant henchmen hesitated. One of them whined, "But it's the Badger."

"I *know* it's the Badger. I can *see* it's the Badger," carped the Under-Stoat. "D'you think I'm bleedin' *blind*? But look about you, lads. There's only one of him, and there's hundreds of us, see? Wotcher waiting for? Follow me!"

The Under-Stoat seized a stick and advanced on the Badger, followed by a dozen soldiers. Badger's great cudgel whistled through the air, and he briefly drove them back. He swung his stick left and right, this way, that way, but scores of other weasels, seeing the great warrior standing alone, gathered up their courage and advanced on him. A moment later, still others followed, until he was covered with weasels, hordes of them, and, despite his stout heart and whirling club, he began to sink beneath their number.

And what of our cake-onauts? What of Matilda? The blood froze in her veins at the sight of Badger disappearing beneath a swarm of weasels, but she willed herself to act. She sprang on a chair and delivered a smart blow to the latch of the cake with her baguette. The three warriors inside—who had been straining against the lid with all their might—poured out, a seeming torrent of Toads, a cascade of Rats, a wave of Moles, all shouting hair-raising war cries that echoed throughout the chamber, magnifying their number into a vast army. They ran to Badger's aid and soon had him dug out. Half the stoats and weasels turned tail and ran to the far end of the hall, shrieking in woe, leaping up the chimney, and hiding under the tables. The other half held the line. It was touch and go.

Badger shouted at Matilda, "Go back to the kitchen and follow that Sammy! He'll know where Humphrey is."

She took off like a shot, clearing a pathway with her bread stick.

⋯⋯⋯

At the far end of the passage off the kitchen, Sammy and Humphrey sat and played a game of chess. Neither's heart was in the game, but for very different reasons. Sammy fidgeted with nerves, while Humphrey sat slumped in apathy. The weasel finally looked at his friend and said, "They have a plan, Humphrey, your uncle and his friends. They're coming to rescue you."

"They are?" said Humphrey, perking up. Then, "Are you going to tell?"

Sammy looked at him. "Why would I do that?"

"I . . . I just thought you might. Since it concerns your tribe, and all."

"You was only good to me, Humphrey. You was my friend."

"Still *am*," vowed Humphrey.

"Nar." Sammy shook his head sadly. "I doubt they'll let us play together again. I'll miss you, I will. And I'll miss our kite. That was the best day I ever had." He sniffled and looked away.

"Then I suppose this is good-bye," said Humphrey, his specs misting up.

"Yeah. I s'pose it is. I'll sit with you until they come. If that's all right with you."

"Yes, please. That would be good."

Shouts filtered down the passage. Soon they could hear the furious cries of the warriors and the thumping of stout staves and the ringing clash of steel.

Humphrey began to quake with nerves. "Oh," he whimpered, "I-I'm afraid."

"Me too," said Sammy. "Me too. Here, give us your paw."

They joined paws and sat side by side. And trembled together. And waited for whatever was to come next.

Fortunately, what came next was Matilda. She rushed into the room and said in urgent tones, "Humphrey, do you know who I am?"

"You're the baker," he whispered. "You winked at me."

"That's right. I'm the baker, and I winked at you. I'm here with your uncle and Rat and Mole and Badger. They're in the great hall at this very moment. Now be a good boy and come with me. There's no need to be afraid. We'll have you home in no time."

Home! Ah, such a lovely word. Such a comforting word. And how it resonated in poor Humphrey's heart. Ah, home! To one who had suffered kidnapping, and false imprisonment, and long days of forced labor, and harrowing nights of loneliness, could there be any more comforting word in the entire language? He let go of Sammy and went to Matilda, but still he hesitated for a moment.

"I've got to go, Sammy," he said.

"You go, Humphrey—'s all right. I'm awful sorry about what happened. You won't hold it against me, will you? I'm awful sorry."

Matilda said, "There's no time. We must hurry."

And although Humphrey's heart was full, and although he had more to say, he wheeled and ran down the passage, Matilda at his side.

A minute later, they had made it to the kitchen. They peeped out into the hall, where our heroes were pushing forward and sweeping all before them. The stoats squealed; the weasels wailed. There was much yelling of the worst kind of profanity: "Drat!" was heard and

"Blast!" and even "By Jove!" and other shocking utterances best not repeated here.

Toad in his fury was puffed up to enormous size; he brandished his stick and screamed like a banshee. Badger, huge and gray, fought in grim silence, all the more terrifying for it. Mole, black and wrathful, laid waste to all in his path. Stouthearted Rat, his fur bristling, pummeled the Under-Stoat and Chief Weasel until they cowered and begged for mercy.

"We give! We give!" they cried, and fell to their knees, weeping.

At the sight of this pitiful display, Badger raised his paw and cried, "Enough! Fall back!" Such was his authority that the others stopped their punishing advance and fell silent.

"I think that they may have had enough," said Badger. "*Have* you had enough, Chief?"

"Oh, yes, oh, yes," wept the Chief.

"Have *you* had enough, Under-Stoat?"

"Oh, Mr. Badger, sir," groveled the Under-Stoat. "Take pity on us. I knows you to be a kind gentleman, sir."

Badger turned to the others and said, "Leave them."

"But, Badger," cried Toad, "let me smack 'em some more! It was my nephew they took, after all. Speaking of which, where is he?"

"I'm over here, Uncle Toad." Humphrey waved from the kitchen.

"Thank goodness, my boy. Are you all right? What a fright you gave us."

"He's fine," called Matilda, and she and Humphrey emerged from the kitchen into the dreadful wreckage of the hall. Tables and chairs were upended; smashed bottles and glasses lay underfoot; squashed sandwiches and great gobs of pulped birthday cake were smeared everywhere.

"Badger's right," said Mole. "They've had enough, don't you think? Let's leave them to their cake and take Humphrey home. Time for a good feed and a nice cup of tea."

"Oh, all right," said Toad. He swung his stick some more and belabored imaginary animals. "You're sure I can't have one more go at them?"

Badger spoke again. "I think," he said slowly, "that we all owe a great debt to the mastermind behind this successful campaign. I am speaking, of course, of Miss Matilda."

"Hear, hear!" cried Ratty. Mole felt an ungracious (and admittedly small-minded) twinge of jealousy deep in the most secret chamber of his heart.

Rat looked at his friend. "I say, Mole, your paw. Is it bleeding?"

"It's nothing," said Mole, stoically pretending it didn't sting like blazes. "Only a flesh wound."

Matilda said, "Let me see that." She inspected the laceration and then tore a strip of clean muslin from her apron. She bandaged the wound with such care and concern that the Mole's pain abated, and he began to think she might not be such a bad sort to have around after all.

"Good old Moly," said Ratty. "Took one for the cause. Splendid fellow!" And with that, the Mole's genial spirits were restored, and he regretted having given way—even briefly—to petty thoughts.

Badger climbed onto the dais, every weasel eye upon him. "Now, look," he said. "Let this be a lesson to you all. Mole, good-hearted chap that he is, has advocated on your behalf, and so we're going to leave you the remains of the cake, although it's more than you deserve. So mind your manners. No more seizing of nephews or, for that matter, young relatives of any kind. Are we clear on that point?"

"Yessir, Mr. Badger." This was accompanied by much bowing and scraping. "Yessir, oh, yessir."

"Now, Mole," Badger went on, "I want you to ride back in the wheelbarrow with Humphrey. You've been wounded, and although it might be just a flesh wound, it still counts. And Humphrey is no doubt exhausted by all the excitement." Upon seeing that the Mole was about to protest, he added, "No guff, now. Get in."

Humphrey, whose knees were shaking so badly that he didn't

trust himself to walk home, was only too glad to be lifted into the barrow after the Mole.

Our party marched up the long hall to the main door. Once outside, they paused to breathe the cool, clear air and rid their lungs of the smoke of battle. Humphrey looked back, and for a second, he saw Sammy peeking around the door at him, forlornly waving good-bye. The next moment the small, bedraggled weasel was yanked away, and the door slammed with a rather rude report.

"It's a shame about the cake," Ratty said to Matilda. "Your grandest creation all smashed up like that."

"Never mind," said Matilda. "It had to be done. I can always bake us another one just like it."

"Well, not *just* like it," said Ratty, to laughter.

They set off for home. Three of our heroes were buoyed up by the success of their mission, and our fourth hero (Rat) was buoyed up by the presence of the fifth hero (Matilda), so none of them minded their fatigue. There was much jocular reliving of critical scenes of the battle and perhaps a bit more self-congratulation than was seemly, but such was only natural in a group of overstimulated animals, and thus could be excused under the circumstances.

Humphrey was naturally disappointed to find that his uncle was no longer a genius, but he was relieved and happy to be rescued.

Finally, at twilight, the weary warriors arrived at the dear old River, that most comforting of landmarks, a sight for the sorest of eyes. They gratefully climbed into the Rat's rowboat and Toad's punt to speed their journey home. Humphrey, exhausted, reclined in the bow and admired the full moon as it rose over the trees. It really was a very full moon. And it really was rising very rapidly. And—how odd—it was giving off an angry buzzing sound.

Just at that second, there was a loud splash between the boats, much too big for a jumping fish, and Humphrey realized with a shock that what he was regarding was not the moon, but in fact Toad's balloon, manned by scores of howling stoats and weasels brandishing muskets and pistols, shaking their fists and bombarding them with a hail of rotten vegetables and stones of worrisome size.

CHAPTER TWENTY-SIX

Ingratitude and Treachery

Or, a weasel's word is only worth the paper it's written on.

Panic! The air whistled with shots; the water leapt with missiles.

"What's happening?" cried Toad, and was immediately splashed in the face when a heavy rock landed a mere foot off the stern.

"Look!" cried Humphrey, momentarily losing sight of the fact that their lives were in peril. He pointed in wonderment at the balloon he'd labored on for so long. "It flies," he said. "Oh, look, Uncle Toad, it flies!"

"We're under attack!" yelled Rat.

"Row, boys, row!" cried Mole.

"I did it!" shouted Humphrey.

"Sit down!" ordered Badger, leaning into his oar and pulling with mighty strokes.

The boats sped downstream in the gathering darkness. Fortunately for our band of warriors, Providence smiled briefly upon them and turned the wind to their benefit, stalling the balloon and allowing them to make the relative safety of the boathouse. They scrambled from their boats and peered upriver at the balloon.

"We've got to get to the Hall," said Badger. "It's our only chance." They looked at the wide expanse of lawn separating them from the security of the stone hall.

"It's awfully far," muttered Toad. "Oh, why did I have to have such a *grand* garden?"

Badger looked at Humphrey, who was really a very squat little toad with very squatty little legs, and said, "Can you run that far?"

Humphrey said, "Um, I can try—"

He was cut off by Badger picking him up and slinging him over his shoulder like a sack of oats. Badger looked at the others and said, "Coming?" Without another word, he wheeled and took off for the hall, Humphrey bouncing on his shoulder with every stride and grimly holding on to his specs.

"Badger's right," said Matilda. "We've got to make a dash for it." She tucked up her skirts and said, "It's our only chance. Look out! The wind is turning!"

Sure enough, fickle Fortune, which had so kindly smiled on them just moments before, now whimsically bestowed her favors on the enemy. The balloon drifted toward them at a fair clip. Rat and Mole and Matilda and Toad looked at one another and then bolted after Badger and his burden, running at top speed. A great chorus of jeers and cat-calls and pistol shots from the heavens marked their progress. Toad, furious at having to make a run for it across his own front lawn, paused briefly to make rude gestures and shout unprintable insults, but all he got for his trouble was a direct hit from an ancient tomato and a near miss from an elderly cabbage.

"Look what you've done to my waistcoat!" Toad shouted. "Rotten tomato all over it! You'll pay for this, you will!"

Came the replies: "Ha, Toady, not so grand now!" "Yar!" "Prat!"[83]

By this time, the others had made it to the shelter of the grand stone portico and were jumping up and down and waving and screaming, "Toad!" "There's no time!" "Run!"

A pistol shot raised a clump of turf just inches from his toes, which caused him to reconsider his need for a promise of payment of his cleaning bill. He sprinted the last thirty yards at an impressive speed, despite the fact that his progress was hampered by a vicious rain of root vegetables falling down upon him.

---

83. Oh, dear. This is such a very rude insult that it pains me to translate it, and I think we should just get on with our story.

"I thought you were a goner, Uncle Toad," said Humphrey.

"Don't be silly, my boy," he panted. "There's not a weasel born yet that's got the better of old Toad. Why, I can remember during the great Battle of Toad Hall—"

Ratty said, "There's no time for reminiscence. If I'm not mistaken, they're heading for the roof."

They looked up to see the great airship floating toward the battlements.

Toad said, "I must say, they're doing quite a decent job of navigating, considering you can't actually steer it and all. Why, it took me days of practice to—"

"Oh, do shut up, Toady," said Rat.

"Enough of this," said Badger. "Everyone inside. We'll have to make a stand on the roof."

Rat said to Matilda, "I want you to take Humphrey to his room and lock the door. Don't come out until one of us comes to get you."

They rushed into the hall and ran smack into the agitated butler with the anxious cook and scullery mouse hard on his heels. "Go to the wine cellar," ordered Badger. "Lock yourselves in and don't come out until we give the all-clear. Understood?"

They looked uncertainly at their master, who nodded and said, "We're under ambush by stoats and weasels on the roof. Dozens—

no, scores—no, hundreds of 'em! I'd do what Mr. Badger said, if I were you."

The servants blanched and scuttled away. The warriors hurried to the weapons room. Matilda and Humphrey started up the stairs, but the young toad halted their progress and said, "Wait, I've an idea, but we have to go to the kitchen first."

"This is no time to be thinking of food," chided Matilda.

"I'm not thinking of food," he said. "I'm thinking of a weapon." He wheeled and ran for the kitchen. The mystified Matilda had no choice but to follow.

Our heroes, meanwhile, had reached the weapons room. They threw open the doors and were confronted with an enormous confusion of weapons of every sort, both modern and ancient, all jumbled together in a huge, untidy pile. They surveyed the twisted mound of pikes and halberds and crossbows.

"Er," said Toad, "I've been meaning to get to this."

Badger waded into the pile and pulled out a terrifying battle-ax. Mole followed suit and selected an evil-looking mace. Ratty pulled out a brace of gleaming pistols and stuck them in his belt. Toad, perhaps thinking of his pirate days, selected a long, glittering sword. He tested it by slicing the air, once, twice—*whish, whish*—and said, "How terribly satisfying."

"No more playing about," said Badger. "Everyone ready?"

"Rightio," said Ratty.

"To the roof!" cried Mole.

"No quarter given," added Toad, working himself into a frenzy. "The nerve of that lot. Landing on my very own roof in my very own balloon. I'll show 'em a thing or two. Or three or four!"

They dashed for the stairs, their footsteps ringing on the flagstones. They trotted across the landing, where they crossed paths with Humphrey and Matilda, who were dashing in another direction.

"Where are you going?" cried Ratty without stopping. "What's that you've got?"

"No time," Matilda yelled, and she and Humphrey ran down the long hall to his room. They threw their burdens onto the bed. Matilda locked the door while Humphrey pushed books and tools off the window seat, clearing a working space. "Hand me that length of pipe," he said.

The forgotten kite, drooping in the corner, looked down silently on their frantic preparations.

Our band of four continued up the stairs, up past the guest floors, up past the nursery, up past the servants' quarters.

"Oh," puffed Toad, "why must there be so many flights of stairs? Why must I have such a *grand* house? I vow to live a simpler life from now on."

"Stop complaining," said Ratty, "and keep up."

They came at last to the attic, a vast gloomy space, and paused momentarily to catch their breath and adjust their weapons. Then it was time. They put their shoulders to the roof door.

"Ready?" whispered Badger. "On three."

The Rat thought of Matilda downstairs and wondered if he would ever see her face again, and touch his nose to hers.

"One."

The Mole thought of the River and wondered if he would ever again drift along in the tiny blue-and-white boat, a good book in hand.

"Two."

The Badger thought of his snug familiar burrow and wondered if he would ever again sit before the fire on a winter's eve, warming his slippered feet before the dying coals and drowsing over a mug of hot cocoa.

"Three!"

The Toad, who was only just beginning to collect his thoughts, did not have time to think of much, for by that point, they were tearing through the door.

Before them lay the open space of the roof, and there was the cannon, kept in good repair for firing on the Queen's Birthday. Hovering just above it was the great balloon, overflowing with the enemy, all shrieking at fever pitch. Their howls grew even louder when they saw the heroes on the battlements. A rope ladder dangled from the balloon, and the first of them scrambled down it.

"They mustn't take the cannon," cried Badger. "It's all over if they take the cannon." The four warriors rushed across the roof and were met by a fusillade of musket fire, forcing them to take cover behind a bulwark of chimneys. They watched helplessly as the enemy poured onto the roof.

"What'll we do?" cried Toad.

"We have to wait until they've fired all their ammunition," said Rat. "Then we'll advance."

Mole whipped off his coat, followed by the Canary Mélange waistcoat, which he then hoisted on the point of his sword. It was instantly pocked with musketry fire, and a few moments later, they could hear the clicking of the weasel's empty guns.

"Good work," said Rat. "I'll get you a new one when this is all over."

Mole looked at his shredded waistcoat and said, "Never mind. It wasn't really me."

"Advance!" cried Badger, and the four leapt from their hiding place and ran at the enemy.

Toad found himself face-to-face with the Under-Stoat and shouted, "*En garde!*"

The Under-Stoat snickered. "You always was so pretentious, Toad. Time to take you down a peg."

"Pretentious?" cried the outraged Toad. "I'll show you pretentious!" He saluted his foe, his sword *whish*ing through the air, and the roof was instantly changed into the deck of the HMS *Amphibia*, the Under-Stoat transformed into the Imaginary Fiend. The admiral lunged at the Fiend and thrust and parried, and drove him back to a turret, and was in turn driven back to a chimney. Back and forth the battle raged, but this time there was no Imaginary Parrot to tilt the scales.

The Rat, who was holding off a good handful of stoats, looked up to see several others reach the cannon. They began to swivel it toward the thick of the fray. "Stop them!" he yelled.

Things looked very black indeed. But just at that moment, Humphrey charged through the attic door carrying a strange contraption that looked like a length of pipe. Matilda was right behind him with a flaming torch.

"Stand back," Humphrey cried, and dropped to one knee, hoisting the pipe over his shoulder. "Load!"

Matilda pushed a shiny missile into the weapon's maw.

"Fire!"

Matilda lit the fuse and covered her ears, and a terrible noise— *FOOM!*—rent the air.

From the mouth of the mortar flew a shiny tin, spewing a jet of dark gold liquid, covering the invaders from head to foot.

They stopped in their tracks and looked curiously at the viscous stuff slowly trickling down them. They sniffed at the strange substance. One or two of the bravest among them tentatively licked at it. It looked like—it smelled like—it *was*—treacle. And just as it dawned on them that they were now covered with the stickiest substance known to man or beast, Humphrey again cried, "Load!" Matilda stuffed a new fuse into one end of the mortar and what appeared to be a pillow in the other.

"Fire!" cried Humphrey. Another terrible *FOOM!* split the night, and now the air was inexplicably filled with snow, fat white flakes that drifted gently down and covered the enemy.

But the snow was not snow. It was feathers.

And there they stood, a sticky packet of stoats/weasels, bonded together and frozen in place. Stuck fast, glued as one, treacled and feathered.[84]

Oh, such heartrending screams of distress as had never before been heard on the Riverbank. "Oh! Oh!" yelled the *klumpf.* And "Ow!

---

84. The author is disappointed to find that there is no specific word in the dictionary for a solid clump of Mustelidae frozen in place with treacle. The author, therefore, begs the reader's indulgence and proposes the adoption of a new word to describe such a group: *klumpf.*

Ow!" they cried, for nothing so upsets and pains a weasel as sticky fur. "We give! We give!"

"You said that before," Toad reminded them. "Why should we believe you now?"

" 'Cos we really means it this time, Mr. Toad. We're awful sorry."

They sobbed on and on, and cried copious floods of tears. So desperately downhearted were they, so wretchedly miserable, that even Toad, in all his injured pride, felt a wave of pity wash over him.

"All right," said Badger. "That's enough. But for your punishment, you're going to have to stand there all night long. We'll send up some soap and hot water in the morning."

"Look," said Mole, pointing to the sky as the balloon, now without cargo or pilot, floated serenely away.

"Drat," said Toad. "Do you think we could—"

"No," said Badger. "Now come on, you lot. Time for a cuppa."

Our heroes repaired to the drawing room, and this time, the accolades were all for Humphrey, who had saved the day with his magnificent invention.

"My boy," said Toad, "you are the true genius in the family. Fancy thinking of a thing like that, and under such perilous pressure, I might add. I'm proud of you." He then spoke in a lowered voice. "I say, you wouldn't teach me how to make one of those mortar things, would you?"

"No, Uncle Toad."

Toad whispered, "Perhaps you'd leave me some of that powder when you go back to school?"

"No, Uncle Toad."

"Not even a little bit?"

"No."

"Toad," snapped Badger, "whatever you're whispering about, stop it. Give us our tea. We're all parched."

"Miss Matilda," said Toad, "will you do the honors?"

Matilda poured the tea, all the while watched fondly by Ratty. Mole noted this, and saw how the one completed the other, and realized that what would be, would be.

Conversation gradually trailed away, and a contented silence fell over the room, unbroken except for the occasional pop from the fireplace.

On the roof above, the klumpf stood motionless through the night and had many long hours to think repentant thoughts.

CHAPTER TWENTY-SEVEN

How It All Turned Out

In which we come to the end of our tale, as we must.

Reader, you may ask at this point, What of our cast of characters? Well, because you have been steadfast and made it this far, I shall tell you.

The balloon was never seen again. Toad generously gave the reward to Humphrey and Sammy as promised, even though the manner of its return had not exactly gone as anticipated.

Humphrey returned to boarding school and excelled in science, especially in his physics class, where he was allowed—even encouraged—to build rockets and mortars and trebuchets.[85] He came up with a new design for a potato cannon that markedly improved both accuracy and distance, thus establishing him as a favorite with his form mates. He extracted from his uncle a promise that he could spend the following summer at Toad Hall, with the stipulation that there would be no more swimming lessons.

Sammy would join Humphrey on the lawn when he was able to get away from minding his brothers and sisters, and together they built elaborate kites and paper airplanes, and even an ornithopter[86] powered by a rubber band, which completely confounded the local birds, especially the know-it-all Swift.

For months, Toad did nothing more than potter about in the garden and conservatory. He took up orchid growing, he took up lawn bowls. He even tried to read a book. He really did try to live the quiet life, but of course it didn't take, and he began to make secret inquiries about the requirements for a license to operate an airplane, taking great pains that Ratty and Mole not find out.[87]

---

85. A trebuchet is a large catapult invented in medieval times. It is useful for hurling heavy objects, such as watermelons.

86. Ornithopter: an aircraft that has wings like a bird, and flies by flapping them up and down.

87. He is still waiting to receive word back from the authorities, which makes one wonder if they're not aware of his reputation regarding machinery.

Badger returned to his extensive warren and spent most of his days enjoying his own company. Every Sunday, the Rat and Mole appeared at his door for a cup of tea, and many an evening was spent telling and retelling the Skirmish of the Birthday Cake, along with the Battle of Treacle and Feathers, both of which gradually passed into legend.

Rat and Matilda were married in style at Toad Hall, Toad giving the bride away and Mole serving as best man. After returning from their honeymoon, they set up housekeeping together, with Ratty pitching in to help with special bakery orders whenever he was needed. A few months later, Mole, now a regular visitor for supper, noticed that Matilda was gaining weight beneath her apron, which he chalked up to the occupational hazard of being a baker. Imagine his surprise when he visited a few days later, and there in seven tiny baskets lay seven tiny rats, each one named for a day of the week. Mole naturally felt a bit excluded at first, what with the new parents being so busy with their offspring. But then Ratty and Matty asked him to be godfather to their litter, an honor that overwhelmed the Mole, who took his duties very seriously. He shepherded the children to and from the River. He helped Ratty teach them to swim and row and fish; he kept them from tickling the dabbling ducks' chins too unmercifully.

One afternoon, tiny Wednesday took him by the paw and said, "Uncle Mole, will you please read me a story? Please?"

"I certainly will," said Mole. "What shall we read?" He ran his paw along the bookshelf. So many wonderful stories to choose from! He paused at the book about the girl falling down the rabbit hole; he considered the boy who was pursuing buried treasure; he lingered over the jungle boy raised by a great furry bear. Then he chose his favorite story of all: the story of a mole who, burdened with spring cleaning, throws his brush and whitewash pail aside, scrapes and scrabbles his way up to the meadow, and there meets a water rat, who introduces him to the joys of the River life.

"Look here," he said to the baby. "Here's my favorite. It's about a couple of dear old friends and their sunny days together spent messing about in boats. Would you like to hear this one?"

"Yes, please," said Wednesday. Mole sat in an overstuffed armchair and she curled up expectantly beside him. He opened the book to the first page and began to read, and knew his happiness to be complete.

THE END

ACKNOWLEDGMENTS

Thanks to my husband, Rob Duncan, for his support and suggestions during the writing of this book. (He is, fortunately, a fan of the original.) Thanks to my parents, especially to my mother, for her excellent proofreading skills. Thanks to my writing group, The Fabs of Austin: Pansy Flick, Nancy Gore, Gaylon Greer, Jim Haws, Kim Kronzer, Diane Owens, and Lottie Shapiro. Thanks to my friends and relatives, Gwen Erwin, Elizabeth Sutherland, Val Brown, Lee Ann Urban, Carol Jarvis, Noeleen Thompson, Gary Cooke, and Robin Allen, for their support and comments.

Thanks to Nigel "Badger" McMorris and the Kenneth Grahame Society, along with Rangi Ruru Girls' School in Christchurch, New Zealand. Thanks to Dr. Joan Lasenby, Fellow of Trinity College, University of Cambridge.

Thanks to Paula Corey and Julie Dunlap for allowing me the use of their lovely garden in Santa Fe, and to Lynne Roberts and Laurie Sandman for making this possible. Thanks to James and Lou Ann Bradley for the use of their cabin in the mountains.

In writing this book, I sought the help of various experts. I hasten to add that any information I may have got wrong is entirely my fault, and not theirs. Thanks to Mr. Robert Noel, Lancaster Herald of the College of Arms, London, for advice regarding Toad's coat of arms; to Mr. John Baker, Archivist, British Balloon & Airship Club, for advice on Toad's balloon; to Mr. Ian Reinhardt, Catering Manager of Trinity College, Cambridge, for information regarding Toad's postprandial wine. Thanks to Special Agents Byron San Marco, Shawn Kang, and Doug Kunze of the Austin, Texas, office of the Bureau of Alcohol, Tobacco, Firearms, and Explosives, for their advice on pyrotechnics and constructing a mortar. Those readers who are actually interested in building a mortar (just a small one, now), or a trebuchet or potato cannon, are referred to *Backyard Ballistics* by William Gurstelle.

Thanks to my editor, Laura Godwin, and Kate Butler and April Ward at Henry Holt Books for Young Readers, and thanks to my agent, Marcy Posner of Folio Literary Management. Thanks to Clint G. Young, for his wonderful new illustrations, and to the Austin chapter of the Society of Children's Book Writers and Illustrators, for introducing us.

And, of course, my eternal gratitude to the peerless Kenneth Grahame, whose immortal tale of friendship has enchanted so many readers, in so many lands, for so many years. We will meet him at the River, where he lives on forever.